PENGUIN

THE DIARY OF LA[

MURASAKI SHIKIBU was born in Japan *c.* 973, during the Heian period (794–1192), when the head of the major faction of the Fujiwara clan, Michinaga, held sway over the imperial court. Her father was a minor official, who never became more than a provincial governor, and whose chief claim to fame must be his role in the education of his remarkable daughter. Apart from what she reveals in her diary, we know little of her life. She married around the turn of the century, had one daughter and was widowed soon after. During the next four or five years Murasaki seems to have begun writing *The Tale of Genji*, the work of fiction that was to bring her fame. It is probable that chapters were read at court and came to the notice of Michinaga, who decided that she would be an excellent addition to the entourage of his daughter, Shōshi (or Akiko), the young emperor's first consort. She entered the service of Shōshi in 1006. Her diary describes the details of court life, the birth of a prince, and contains some tart observations on her contemporaries, but the record as we have it today does not go beyond 1010. Lady Murasaki is best known as the author of the *Genji*, a long prose narrative of astonishing complexity and sophistication, which is today recognized as one of the masterpieces of Japanese literature. It is not known exactly how long she lived, but she probably died at some time between 1014 and 1025.

RICHARD BOWRING was educated at Downing College, Cambridge. He subsequently taught at Monash, Columbia and Princeton, returning to Cambridge in 1985 as Professor of Japanese Studies. In 2000 he was elected Master of Selwyn College. His books include *Mori Ōgai and the Modernization of Japanese Culture* (1979) and *A Student Guide: Murasaki Shikibu, The Tale of Genji* (1988; 2nd edn, 2004). He is also co-author of *An Introduction to Modern Japanese* (1992) and *Cambridge Intermediate Japanese* (2002), and co-editor of *The Cambridge Encyclopedia of Japan* (1993). His primary research is now in the field of Japanese religions.

# The Diary
# of Lady Murasaki

*Translated and introduced by*
RICHARD BOWRING

PENGUIN BOOKS

PENGUIN BOOKS

Published by the Penguin Group
Penguin Books Ltd, 80 Strand, London WC2R ORL, England
Penguin Group (USA) Inc., 375 Hudson Street, New York, New York 10014, USA
Penguin Books Australia Ltd, 250 Camberwell Road, Camberwell, Victoria 3124, Australia
Penguin Books Canada Ltd, 10 Alcorn Avenue, Toronto, Ontario, Canada M4V 3B2
Penguin Books India (P) Ltd, 11 Community Centre, Panchsheel Park, New Delhi – 110 017, India
Penguin Group (NZ), cnr Airborne and Rosedale Roads, Albany, Auckland 1310, New Zealand
Penguin Books (South Africa) (Pty) Ltd, 24 Sturdee Avenue, Rosebank 2196, South Africa

Penguin Books Ltd, Registered Offices: 80 Strand, London WC2R ORL, England

www.penguin.com

First published 1996
Reprinted with corrections 2005

039

Set in 10/12.5 pt Monotype Bembo
Typeset by Datix International Limited, Bungay, Suffolk

Printed and bound in Great Britain by Clays Ltd, Elcograf S.p.A.

ISBN-13: 978–0–14–043576–4

www.greenpenguin.co.uk

*For Marian Ury – in memoriam*

# CONTENTS

# PREFACE

This book is a re-edited and revised version of the author's earlier work *Murasaki Shikibu: Her Diary and Poetic Memoirs* (Princeton: Princeton University Press, 1982), which has been out of print for some years. The revision has involved a number of major changes, not the least of which has been the decision to omit the collection of poetry (*Murasaki Shikibu shū*). Such is the nature of these short, largely conventional, poems that their inclusion in a book destined for a wide audience would probably end in puzzlement rather than pleasure or enlightenment, even if the task were attempted by a more able translator of poetry than myself. Annotations that dealt with specialized textual problems have also been omitted. A more general set of introductory essays has been supplied, although it is tempting just to guide the reader in the direction of Ivan Morris's *The World of the Shining Prince* (Kōdansha International, 1994), which covers a lot more ground with a good deal more wit and style. The translation of the diary itself has been extensively revised in the light of comments by reviewers of the earlier book, further study of recent Japanese commentaries, and a reading of the French translation by René Sieffert, which was a belated discovery. I cannot speak for its style, which seems consciously archaic, but it is a work of impeccable and impressive accuracy. For the footnotes I make no apology. They are an absolute necessity when translating a work of this nature, which was written with the unstated assumption that the reader would already have extensive background knowledge of the culture and the times.

# A NOTE ON JAPANESE
# NAMES AND DATES

## *Names*

All Japanese names in this book are presented in conventional Japanese order: family, or clan, name first (for example, Fujiwara) and personal name second (for example, Michinaga). In the period concerned, it was the custom to insert the particle *no*, signifying 'of', between the two names. I have retained its use, although this custom seems to have died out after about 1200.

Readers will find that men, in particular, are identified in the translation sometimes by title, sometimes by name and sometimes by both. In the original Japanese one finds only titles, and quite often the same person is identified by different titles in different places, even in the course of what is a very short narrative. Occasionally it is clear why one title has been used in preference to another in a particular context, but this is not always the case. Where possible, I have tried to retain the use of titles, but personal names have been added where necessary. The translation of titles, with very few exceptions, follows those set out in the detailed appendices to William H. and Helen Craig McCullough, trans., *A Tale of Flowering Fortunes* (Stanford: Stanford University Press, 1980).

The only women to be given personal names in the diary are servants. Ladies-in-waiting are usually identified by a combination of rank, or position, with a name derived from the title or land-holding of a near male relative. This was necessary because a number of women might hold a specific title, hence they needed an additional label. I have followed convention and by and large simply transliterated rather than translated these names. Ben no Naishi, for example, was a handmaid (*naishi*), whose father or husband held (or had held) the rank of Controller (*ben*) in the Council of State. The term 'Lady' has been used freely and subsumes a number of distinct but ill-understood female titles. The author's real name (if such a concept would have meant anything to her) is unknown. 'Lady Murasaki' translates, or rather stands for, Murasaki Shikibu. This is a combination of a nickname – Murasaki – which refers to the main female character in her major fiction *Genji monogatari* ('The Tale of Genji'), and the name of a ministry – Shikibu or 'Ministry of Ceremonial' – in which her father had once held a post.

## Dates

The Western (Julian) calendar and the Japanese calendar do not co-incide, with the result that conversion of dates is no easy matter. The Japanese had days and months, as one might expect from a lunar calendar, but years were calculated in 'eras', and a change of era name might be precipitated by anything from an epidemic to an omen. Era names were not linked to emperors' reigns until the modern period. The convention followed here is: a date written Kankō 5 (1008).7.16 signifies the sixteenth day of the seventh month of the year Kankō 5. This equates to 20 August 1008 in the Julian calendar, but since in this context it is not usually relevant to know the precise Western equivalent, most dates have been left unconverted except for the guide as to the year in question, which appears in brackets. The reader should be aware, however, that although this system works fairly well for most of the calendar year in question, it does not work if the date falls near the beginning or the end of the year, when the rule-of-thumb equation fails. Kankō 3, for example, is usually marked as 1006, but Kankō 3.12.29, when we think Murasaki first entered court service, was actually 20 January, 1007. To translate it as such, however, would only confuse matters, because to Murasaki herself it represented the penultimate day of the year.

# INTRODUCTION

## Cultural Background

### GENERAL

Lady Murasaki, or Murasaki Shikibu as she is known in Japanese, lived at the height of the Heian Period (794–1192), a long era of relative peace and stability, which takes its name from the capital, Heian-kyō ('Capital of Peace and Tranquillity'), the ancestor of what is now the city of Kyōto. Japan was emerging from a period of intense absorption of Chinese material and written culture, during which alien concepts such as the centralization of power, the role of bureaucracy, and the mysteries of Buddhist philosophy were first imported and then gradually naturalized. The court decided as early as 894 to abandon the practice of sending official embassies to China, partly because the T'ang dynasty was already in terminal decline and partly because a willing ambassador could not be found. The last Korean goodwill mission visited Japan in 928. By the time of Murasaki's birth in *c.* 973, therefore, Japan had turned in upon itself. What had been imported had by this stage been well digested and we can begin to see the main outlines of subsequent Japanese culture emerging. Murasaki's own monumental work, the *Genji monogatari* ('Tale of Genji') was, therefore, the product of a native culture, enriched by Chinese example, finding a truly sophisticated form of self-expression for the first time. China was, of course, to remain as a kind of touchstone, but it was geographically and psychologically remote enough to allow the unhampered growth of an indigenous tradition.

This shift away from things Chinese occurred not only in literature and religion but also in politics and government. Early attempts to impose a Chinese-style bureaucracy never really succeeded in supplanting native habits, and power remained very much a matter of heredity. At court, the Emperor stood at the spiritual centre, but he was politically impotent and was usually under the influence of whichever aristocratic family happened to be in a position to force decisions. The Emperor's daily existence was largely involved with ritual, and his links to the actual machinery of government were extremely tenuous. He was, in any case, often too young and inexperienced to be able to have a mind of his own. The coveted post in the system was that of Regent, the degree of power being directly related to the proximity of Regent to Emperor as measured through family ties. It is only to be expected then that 'marriage politics' should have emerged as a major technique whereby power was gained and then maintained.

In Murasaki's day the court was dominated by one clan, the Fujiwara, and in particular by one branch, the Northern Branch, and by one man, Fujiwara no Michinaga (966–1027). His chief asset was a carefully designed network of marriage ties, which he manipulated to great effect. He was also lucky in matters of births and deaths. Such a position of prominence was only achieved as the result of much internecine strife between various family factions vying for power throughout the late tenth century. Rivalry within the Fujiwara clan itself came to a head in 969, when the major remaining threat from a different clan, Minamoto no Takaakira (914–82), was finally removed from the scene on a trumped-up charge of conspiracy. From that time on there ensued a series of intrigues that set brother against brother, nephew against uncle, and that led to the early demise of three emperors, Reizei, En'yū and Kazan. A typical example is that of Kazan (r. 984–6), who was sixteen at the time of his accession. Under strong pressure from Fujiwara no Kaneie, who wanted to put his grandson, later Emperor Ichijō, on the throne, he was eventually tricked into taking orders and thus relinquishing authority. Ichijō (r. 986–1011), who reigned during the time of most interest to us in the present context, came to the throne at the age of six and was naturally dominated by his grandfather. Kaneie had three sons, Michitaka (953–95), Michikane (961–95), and Michinaga (966–1027). When Kaneie died in 990, he was initially replaced by Michitaka, who immediately proceeded to consolidate his position by making his daughter, Teishi, Imperial Consort and promoting his son Korechika (973–1010) by leaps and bounds in the next few years. But Michitaka died five years later and Michikane followed soon after in an epidemic. Michinaga was now left the job of consolidating his position, and he immediately came into direct conflict with Korechika. It was mainly due to the influence of Michinaga's sister Senshi, Ichijō's mother, that the young Emperor was 'persuaded' to favour his uncle. Only a year later, by a mixture of luck and guile, Michinaga managed to put an end to Korechika's hopes.

The story goes that Korechika, under the impression that retired Emperor Kazan was competing with him for the favours of a certain lady, surprised Kazan one night and started a scuffle in which the retired Emperor was actually winged by an arrow. Whether or not the whole scene had been engineered by Michinaga we do not know, but it provided him with the excuse he needed. Combined with an accusation that Korechika had been trying to place a curse on his uncle, it was enough to have him banished from the court for several months, and from this time on Michinaga proved virtually unassailable. In 999 he introduced his ten-year-old daughter Shōshi (988–1074) to court as Imperial Consort, and she quickly became promoted to Second Empress or *Chūgū*.

In the twelfth month of 1000, Teishi, who had been under considerable pressure since the disgrace of her brother Korechika, died in childbirth, and Shōshi's position became secure. It was into her entourage that Murasaki, from a different and much less important branch of the Fujiwara, was to be introduced as a kind of companion-cum-tutor. As we can tell from her diary and Sei Shōnagon's *Makura no sōshi* ('Pillow Book'), the women's quarters in the Palace were organized around major consorts, and the quality of the cultural 'salon' that each woman could attract was a major factor in their constant rivalry. The real moment of success for Michinaga came when in 1008 Shōshi gave birth to a son, Prince Atsuhira (1008–36). This meant that if all went well Michinaga would be in full control of the next generation. This birth is the main event that Murasaki chronicles in such detail in her diary, hardly surprising in view of the supreme importance of the birth for the faction with which she now found herself involved. It was also a relief to Michinaga, given that the omens had not been very propitious: Shōshi seems to have taken a full nine years to become pregnant.

Michinaga continued to gain influence throughout his career. In the end he could count himself as brother-in-law to two emperors (En'yū and Reizei), uncle to one (Sanjō), uncle and father-in-law to another (Ichijō), and grandfather to two more (Goichijō and Go-suzaku). There is evidence, however, that at this early stage Korechika continued to be a thorn in the flesh, for another scandal erupted in the first month of 1009 when it was 'discovered' that Korechika had arranged for a curse to be laid on Shōshi and the new prince. Korechika was banned from the court again, this time for six months.

It should be clear that women had an important role to play in the politics of the time. They were vital pawns, 'borrowed wombs' as the saying went, and, depending on their strength of character, might wield considerable influence. We know that they had certain rights, income and property that mark them off as being unusually privileged in comparison to women in later ages. Michinaga's mother, for instance, seems to have been a power to be reckoned with, and his main wife Rinshi owned the Tsuchimikado mansion, where he spent so much of his time and which serves as the backdrop for most of the events in Murasaki's diary.

It is much more difficult, however, to determine the true position of women in society at large. The testimony we have from the literature of the period, much of it written by women of a lesser class, draws a picture of women subject to the usual depredations of their menfolk, prey to the torments of jealousy, and condemned to live most of their sedentary lives hidden behind a wall of screens and blinds. Seldom were they known by their own names; they existed rather in the shadow of titles held by brothers and fathers, borrowed labels. Second-ary wives of major figures probably had the worst position, as we can tell from a reading of the *Kagerō nikki* ('Gossamer Years'). The author of this particular autobiographical work was trapped at home, at the mercy of her husband's slightest whim; he had official business and other love affairs to keep him busy. For women like this there were only two escapes – to enter service at court, or to seek solace in

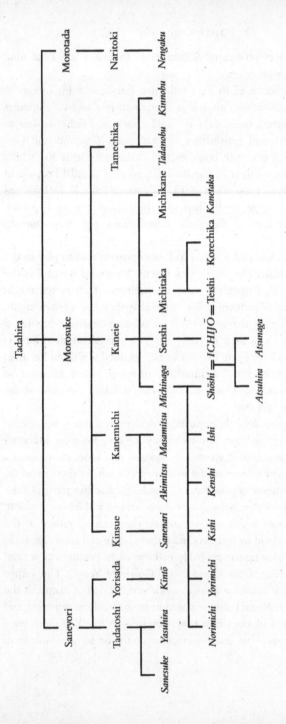

Main members of the Fujiwara clan
[Names mentioned in the diary are in italics]

religion. Murasaki seems to have decided on the first option, which probably came in the form of a request to join Shōshi's entourage; but even so, her diary tells us that life at court was not all it was cracked up to be. Amid a certain magnificence, she also found drunkenness, frivolity, back-biting, and a general sense of life being wasted. We should not, of course, be surprised by any of this. What is truly remarkable is that a number of court women were able to write about their situation in such a fashion that their predicament speaks directly to us today, across barriers of time and place. It is perhaps salutary to remind ourselves that as Murasaki was writing in such exquisite detail of court ceremonial on the one hand and personal feelings on the other, we in England had still full sixty years to go to the Norman Conquest.

## LANGUAGE AND STYLE

The impact of Chinese civilization was felt everywhere in ninth-century Japan but perhaps nowhere more strongly than in matters of language. The Japanese had no writing system of their own prior to their contact with China, so literature itself was a concept learned from Chinese example. By Murasaki's time, written Chinese had been the main vehicle for the bureaucracy for some centuries. By the mid ninth century a syllabary had been developed from a set of Chinese characters used solely for their phonetic value, and this finally led to the growth of written Japanese. In the early stages this was restricted to private correspondence and native poetry. We know from a famous passage in Murasaki's diary that it was still considered unbecoming for a woman to know Chinese, a useful fiction if the intention was to keep the language of bureaucracy in male hands. What this did, however, was to encourage the women to develop written Japanese for their own ends, and in particular for self-expression. So it is that Heian Japan offers us some of the earliest examples of an attempt by women to define the self in textual terms.

Part of the importance of women such as Murasaki is, therefore, their role in the development of Japanese prose. It is sometimes forgotten how difficult a process it is to forge a flexible written style out of a language that has only previously existed in a spoken form. Spoken language assumes another immediate presence and hence can leave things unsaid. Gestures, eye contact, shared experiences and particular relationships all provide a background which allows speech to be at times fragmentary, allusive and even ungrammatical. Written language on the other hand must assume an immediate absence. In order for communication to take place the writer must develop strategies to overcome this absence, this gap between the producer and receiver of the message. The formidable difficulties that most of these texts still present to the modern reader are in large measure attributable not to obscure references (although there are some, of course), nor to deliberate archaisms or what we commonly refer to as 'flowery language', but rather to the fact that the prose has still not entirely managed to break free from its spoken origins.

Murasaki's diary can be read as a kind of testing ground for different styles — three styles, to be exact: first, the kind of factual record one might expect from someone practising to be a chronicler of the time; second, the kind of self-analytical reflection that one might expect of a writer of fiction; and third, a letter to a friend or relative.

We may find the record sections of the diary somewhat tedious, but it is important to remember that such a style and such a subject was still fairly new; records were usually written by men in Sino-Japanese, a hybrid form of writing that was, in a sense, designed for this specific purpose and was certainly far removed from the spoken form of either language. Murasaki was by no means the first to attempt this kind of impersonal, decentred writing in Japanese, but there can be no doubt that it was still in the process of being formed. It was something that had to be practised, something that an aspiring writer in her own native language would have to be able to handle without difficulty. It thus holds an interest and a stylistic importance that is difficult for us to re-create today, especially in translation.

The second style is, if anything, even more important, because without it Murasaki's work would not have the kind of strong appeal it does. Sino-Japanese was so artificial and inflexible a medium that it is difficult to imagine a Japanese of the time being able to use it to express innermost thoughts. Perhaps Fujiwara no Sanesuke (957–1046) in his diary *Shōyūki* comes closest, but still the gap between what he finds himself revealing and what Murasaki can reveal is vast. In this sense, then, Murasaki's diary was another major step, not only for women, but for the language as a whole.

Lastly, whether or not one believes the 'letter' section of the diary to be a real letter or a fictional one, it shows the author dealing with yet another problem: how to maintain a fairly recently developed literary style in a context which closely approached the spoken. This is perhaps the most difficult of the three experiments. Near the end of the letter there are in fact signs that the style is breaking down, degenerating into precisely those disjointed rhythms that are characteristic of speech.

## POETRY

Here and there in the diary, the reader will come across the odd poem or exchange of poems. To an English reader they may seem cryptic in the extreme and somewhat puzzling. A Japanese poem appears at first sight to be little more than a statement thirty-one syllables long. There is no rhyme and no word stress to form the basis of a prosody, so the basic rhythm is provided by an alternating current of 5/7 or 7/5 syllables. The form that we find in the diary, so-called *tanka* or 'short poems', is made up of five such measures: 5/7/5/7/7. There is often a caesura before the final 7/7 but not always. These measures are phrases but not really lines as the term is usually understood, and most Japanese poetry is in fact found written in a single vertical line. It is for this reason that the usual poetic techniques in English cannot be brought into play when attempting a translation. Add to this the fact that much use is made of various kinds of wordplay, intertextual reference, inversion and the like, and it should be obvious why translation is an extremely hazardous affair. Japanese poetry may be short but the result is often a complex weave of words: the texture is the poem.

Poems as short as this do not survive well on their own. Clever statements usually call for some kind of response, otherwise they simply hang there in mid-air. Hardly surprising then to find that poems like these often occur in pairs, their natural habitat being dialogue. They are thus ideally suited to flirtatious banter, used as one of the most important weapons in what we might call a Japanese version of the 'battle of the sexes'. But that is not all. It would appear that the ability to toss off an appropriate poem on any occasion was a *sine qua non* of court life. The number of good poets was probably as limited as it always is, and much of the poetry was certainly mediocre, but it is a commonplace of court societies everywhere that the most ordinary and obvious of activities becomes wrapped in ritual and technique so that essential difference may be preserved and highlighted. Legitimacy, and indeed *raison d'être*, lies within such difference, and what could be more exclusive than the habit of conversing in pairs of cryptic 31-syllable statements? It amounted to a special, artificial dialect. The problem with artificiality of this kind, however, is that it becomes extremely difficult to identify a personal voice behind the strict conventions that grow up around such poetry. Given that much of it was, in any case, meant to be indirect, allusive, and ironic in tone, perhaps it is best to assume that to look for a personal voice is a fool's errand.

## RELIGIOUS BACKGROUND

Although it is extremely doubtful whether Murasaki would have had a concept of 'religion' as a definable area of human experience, she would have certainly recognized the difference between sacred and profane. She would not, however, have seen 'Shintō' and Buddhism as being traditions in any way commensurate. Indeed they managed to coexist precisely because they fulfilled very different needs and so came into conflict but rarely. The use of a term such as 'Shintō' ('Way of the gods') in such a context is in fact anachronistic, because during this period it was neither an organized religion nor a recognizable 'way' to be followed by an individual. The attempt to create a doctrine and so to provide a viable alternative to Buddhism came much later in Japanese history. Shintō was not an intellectual system in any sense. It was rather the practice of certain rituals connected with fertility, avoidance of pollution, and pacification of the spirits of a myriad gods. At the individual level this was not far removed from simple animism, an activity governed by superstition and the need to pacify whatever was unknown, unseen and dangerous. At the level of court and state, however, we find something more formalized, a collection of cults connected to aristocratic families and centred on certain import-ant sites and shrines. Although there did exist formal institutional links between these shrines, in the sense that the government made attempts to put them under some measure of bureaucratic control, they were essentially discrete cults; we cannot, therefore, treat 'Shintō' as a true system. The Fujiwara clan, for example, had its cult centre with its shrine at Kasuga in the Yamato region. This was not linked in any meaningful sense to the shrines at Ise, where the cult centre of the Imperial Family was situated. The Imperial Family sought legitimacy for its rule via the foundation myths propagated in the *Kojiki* ('Record of ancient matters') of 712, but from a Western perspective it is import-ant to understand that this text was mytho-historical in nature, not sacred in the sense of having been 'revealed'. It was not itself of divine origin. It merely explained the origins of Japan and its gods and justi-fied the rule of the Emperor by the simple expedient of linking him directly to these gods. Few could have questioned the story it told; but by the same token it was nothing more than a record of the country's past. The concept of a sacred text does not exist apart from prayers and incantations.

Cult Shintō, if we can call it that without suggesting too much of a system, was therefore linked to matters of public, state and clan ritual rather than private concerns. Of the many centres in Japan, it was those at Ise and at Kamo, just north of the capital, that loomed largest in the consciousness of women such as Murasaki. Both these shrines were central to the legitimacy of the imperial house. There were, of course, others; but these were the most prominent. Ise was by the far the oldest but was also far removed from the capital, linked only by the presence there of the High Priestess of the Ise Shrines, usually a young girl of imperial lineage sent as imperial representative. Few courtiers would have ever been to Ise and most would have had only a very hazy idea of where it lay. Kamo, however, was just north of the capital and within fairly easy access. The institution of High Priestess of the Kamo Shrines was in fact only a fairly recent one, begun in the reign of Emperor Saga in 810. The capital had moved from Nara in 794 and the Imperial Family must have decided that there was a need to create a shrine in the vicinity of the new city. As was the case with Ise, a young girl was chosen to represent the Emperor at the shrine, to ensure the correct rituals were carried out and to maintain ritual purity. Although the intention had been to choose a new girl for every new reign, by Murasaki's time one person, Senshi (964-1035), a daughter of Emperor Murakami, had become a permanent occupant of this post. She held it continuously from 975-1031.

We know from Murasaki's diary, as well as other sources, that Princess Senshi had a formidable reputation as a poet and that she 'held court' at her home near the Kamo shrines. Although Murasaki betrays a certain prickliness at the way this reputation was spread abroad, she nevertheless recognizes Senshi's worth as the leader of a kind of rival literary coterie. We therefore have the somewhat odd spectacle of someone who was supposed to be living in purity and seclusion holding court to visitors of a distinctly secular cast, male as well as female. Perhaps it was for this reason that Sei Shōnagon in her *Pillow Book* considered Kamo to be 'deep in bad karma'.

It happens that not only is Princess Senshi central to one of the main passages in Murasaki's diary but also she provides a good example of the kind of tensions that could exist between Cult Shintō and Buddhism. These traditions are normally thought of as being in total harmony in this period, fulfilling complementary roles. This may well have been the case in many shrine-temple complexes where gods were simply seen as the other side of the Buddhist coin, where every shrine had some sort of Buddhist temple and every temple its protective shrine, but in the restricted world of a place like the Kamo shrines and at Ise, the demands of the two traditions certainly did clash. We know from the collection of Senshi's poetry *Hosshin wakashū* ('Collection of poems for the awakening of faith') that she was constantly torn between the demands of ritual purity, which forced her to avoid contact with all forms of pollution including Buddhism, and her own deeply felt need to find salvation. She was a firm believer in the message of the *Lotus Sūtra* and in Amida as saviour.

Cult Shintō, then, seems to have offered no personal creed, not even for one of its High Priestesses. The impression we get from the literature of the time is that these shrines were not places where an individual would go to pray. Access was usually strictly limited and in most cases remained the prerogative of priests alone. They were sacred sites, where the gods revealed their presence. Once or twice a year public rituals were held, which often took the form of festivals, but the shrines themselves were remote, places of ritual purity whose careful maintenance was essential for natural good order and to ensure future prosperity. It is clear from the case of Princess Senshi that only Buddhism could provide the kind of personal consolation that she needed.[1]

So what of Buddhism at this time? By the tenth century, this import from India and China was firmly entrenched in Japanese court society. It will be noticed, for example, that the majority of the rituals that surround the events in the diary are Buddhist. But there are many forms of Buddhism and the ritual side that we see here is largely tantric in nature. The priests mentioned in the text came from the two major Heian sects, Tendai and Shingon, both of which wielded considerable power. To someone like Murasaki, this is superb, awe-inspiring spectacle with the chanting of sūtras, the burning of incense and quite violent rites of exorcism. It is this kind of ritualized Buddhism that became linked to the native cults via a series of 'identifications' of certain gods with certain Buddhas.

We can tell from Murasaki's diary, however, that there was another kind of Buddhism, the worship of Amida (Amitābha) Buddha. This seemed to answer a more personal need for salvation. Princess Senshi felt the same urge and, despite the tremendous obstacles in her way, chose the same path. Murasaki herself must have been well aware that the Buddhist rituals she saw at court and the path of personal salvation through the worship of Amida were at root connected, but nevertheless one senses a divide. Although we have not yet reached the stage when Amidism becomes to all intents and purposes a monotheistic religion, there can be no doubt that it, and not tantrism, provided the major source of personal solace for these women.

1 On this point see in particular E. Kamens, *The Buddhist Poetry of the Great Kamo Priestess*, Michigan monograph series in Japanese studies: no. 5 (Ann Arbor: University of Michigan, 1990).

## ARCHITECTURE

Much of the 'vagueness' for which Heian literature is supposedly famous stems in large part from a natural assumption of prior knowledge. Take, for example, the word 'palace' as used by Murasaki in this diary. One might expect this to refer to the imposing structure which dominates all formalized maps of the capital, but in fact it refers to a mansion that Emperor Ichijō was forced to use as a substitute because the buildings formally designated as his proper palace had burned down. Ichijō had already been forced to live in a substitute residence twice before, but this was to be the last and the longest of his absences. The main Imperial Palace burned down on Kankō 2 (1005).11.15. He then moved to a number of different buildings before finally settling at the Ichijō mansion on Kankō 3 (1006).3.4. He was to stay here until his abdication and death in 1011, with the exception of the period from Kankō 6 (1009).10.4 to Kankō 7 (1010).11.28, when the Ichijō mansion itself burned down and he had to move to the Biwa mansion. It is this mansion that in fact forms the backdrop for the very last section of Murasaki's diary.

It is useful to remember that for a good portion of his reign, then, Ichijō had to rely mainly on Fujiwara largesse and did not have a proper home base for his activities. The Ichijō mansion was very close to the main palace grounds, near the north-east corner, and belonged to his mother Senshi. His posthumous name came from his association with this mansion, and he may have felt fairly much at home there; but the fact remains that it was a Fujiwara possession. The move to the Biwa mansion – so named after the loquat trees (*biwa*) in the gardens – must have been even more restricting; this residence was much further to the east in what can only be called the 'Fujiwara quarter' of the city, and it had come into Michinaga's possession in 1002. During this period, then, the Emperor was living under his father-in-law's roof.

The diary opens with an autumn scene at the Tsuchimikado mansion. This belonged to Michinaga's wife Rinshi, but Michinaga himself started to use it as his principal residence from around 991. It did not become his property as such until much later, when in 1016–17 he paid for its reconstruction after yet another disastrous fire. It occupied a large area (two 'blocks', 2493 × 1187 metres) in the far north-east corner of the capital. It was here that Michinaga's daughter, Empress Shōshi, came to give birth. Partly this was to avoid the strict taboo on the shedding of blood in the precincts of the Imperial Palace (or what stood for them), but it must have also presented Michinaga with a marvellous opportunity to show off his wealth and power. Murasaki's description of the occasion of the Imperial visit to the mansion to see Shōshi and the new baby, when he was hardly given any time together with her ('The Emperor went in to see Her Majesty, but it was not long before there were shouts that it was getting late and that the palanquin was ready to leave'), shows just how much Ichijō was at the mercy of protocol and bereft of any say in his own activities.

Domestic architecture of the period was very distinctive, and it is important for the reader of Murasaki's diary to be aware of its main features. To understand a particular action, or indeed a particular emotional reaction, one must know where people are sitting, what the building looks like, and what the people are looking at. The mansions themselves were only rarely more than one storey high but they covered a large area; a series of rectangular buildings linked by covered walkways, the central structure being by far the largest. The whole residence would be enclosed by walls with entrance gates on at least three sides. The main buildings would lie to the north with wings east and west extending out into the gardens, which lay to the south. All construction was of wood, with bark rather than tiled roofs. The base was raised on thick stilts about one or two feet high to provide as much airflow as possible during the semi-tropical summer months and because of the generally damp atmosphere of Japan. The architecture was open, numerous pillars supporting a large expanse of roof on elaborate trusses. The roof line would sweep down well beyond the pillars so forming an extra protected area skirting the building. Outside that there would be a veranda. Inner space was divided from outer sometimes by wooden walls but for the most part by a series of removable screens. These were designed so that the top half could be swung up; the bottom half needed more effort because it had to be removed in its entirety. Behind this there would be a layer of blinds and perhaps curtains. The core characteristic of these buildings was that the

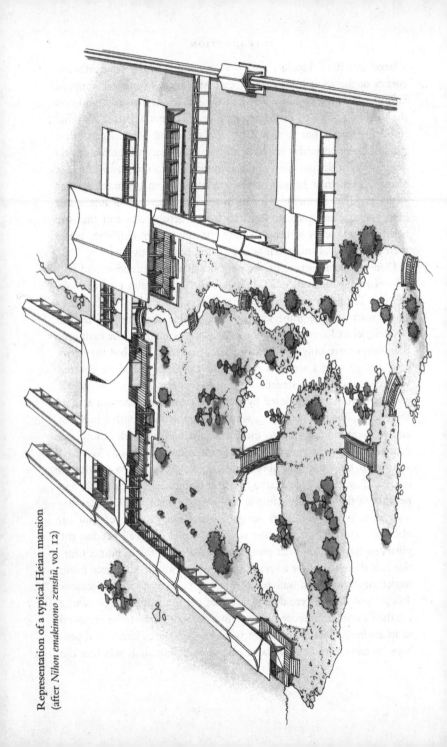

Representation of a typical Heian mansion
(after *Nihon emakimono zenshū*, vol. 12)

boundary between outside and inside was fluid in the extreme, with a design of utmost flexibility. The one drawback was of course their vulnerability to the inclement weather. They must have been unbearably cold in winter with no protection from the wind and little to warm one but a small brazier. It is hardly surprising that these buildings burned down with depressing regularity.

The lack of a sense of boundary was reflected inside as well, where a 'room' might well consist of nothing more than a 'tent' of curtains. At busy times one's room might even have to be set up in the corridor that skirted round the outside. Privacy in such an environment was impossible, especially as the space above the 'room' divisions must have been open to the roof, with all that meant for overhearing conversations. The floors were usually bare wood with the occasional mat. The modern Japanese *tatami* mat that covers the whole floor and 'gives' a little had not yet been invented. Furniture was minimal. By and large the interior of this large space must have been extremely dark, and the inhabitants for at least half the year had to wear many layers of clothing to keep warm. It is these clothes that became the subject of near-fetishistic concern with the ladies-in-waiting. Most of the women spent most of the time either sitting or kneeling on the floor, and their bed would be a thin mat simply rolled out. A man standing outside in the garden looking in, therefore, would have had the railings of the veranda at about mid-height and his eyes would have been roughly level with the skirts of the women inside.

It is clear from Murasaki's diary that she was extremely interested in her surroundings. This may partly be a false impression produced by a desire to describe positions accurately for the sake of the record, but even so one cannot help being struck by the degree to which the author is aware of position and placing within this large residence. There are general links here, of course, to a cultural obsession with hierarchy and status, but it is of interest that the cardinal points of the compass are very clear in the mind of the writer. They help give a specificity to the descriptions. From one angle the fact that we need plans and drawings to understand what is going on in certain sections of the diary can be seen as a criticism. From another angle, however, it is truly remarkable that we can in fact create accurate plans on the basis of her record. If her aim was to practise building up a word-picture of a historical event in all its concreteness, the experiment must be judged a brilliant success.

## DRESS

No one could fail to remark on the extent to which Murasaki concentrated on her descriptions of dress. The detail here too is at times almost suffocating. Clearly, concerns with colour combinations and types of fabric and weave were close to a fetish in court circles. This went beyond the usual concern with what might or might not be allowed: taste in clothes was obviously a major indicator of character and style, one of the ways in which a lady-in-waiting could make her mark and show her individuality. It is again difficult to gauge whether such detail was present simply because Murasaki wished to produce as close a record of an event as possible or whether she herself was obsessed with such details for other reasons. Be that as it may, it is important to have as clear a picture as possible as to what these dresses looked like. As the illustration indicates, we should not try to visualize the modern kimono with its tight, wide belt held high over the breasts. The clothing worn by Heian court women was much looser, much longer and in many more layers. There was a basic white under-garment and a pair of long trouser-skirts, *nagabakama*, usually red, which formed the basis for the following:

(i) A simple unlined dress (*hitoe*)

(ii) A set of lined robes of various colours and combinations (*itsutsuginu* or *[kasane]uchigi*)

(iii) A gown, often of crimson beaten silk (*uchiginu*)

(iv) A mantle (*uwagi*), the lining of which often protruded beyond the surface at the sleeve openings

(v) A train (*mo*)

(vi) A jacket (*karaginu*). For less formal occasions the train and jacket would be replaced by an informal outer robe (*kouchigi*).

The material used for *uwagi, mo* and *karaginu* was known as *orimono* (figured silk), a general term that seems to have included most of the

Formal court attire for a Heian-lady-in-waiting

1 Trouser skirts (*nagabakama*)
2 Unlined dress (*hitoe*)
3 Lined robes (*itsutsuginu* or
    *[kasane]uchigi*)
4 Gown (*uchiginu*)
5 Mantle (*uwagi*)
6 Train (*mo*)
7 Jacket (*karaginu*)

heavy patterned silks such as brocade (*nishiki*), ribbed (*kanhata*), embroidered (*nuimono*), damask (*aya*) and taffeta (*katori*). *Karaginu*, however, if Murasaki's diary is anything to go by, could sometimes be made of thin transparent gauze.

The lined robes were usually of very thin material, gauzes and gossamers, known by the generic term *usumono*. These robes were given most attention in descriptions because it was here that the colour combinations of outer material and inner lining came into play. As the upper layer was gauze, the colour of the lining shone through, producing a third composite colour, which was referred to by a single term, usually the name of a flower. Dark red shining through white produced 'plum blossom', and light purple beneath white produced 'cherry blossom', and so forth. It should be remembered that although the passages containing descriptions of women's dresses are obviously of major importance to the author, the translation is often tentative: there is not always a consensus on the precise match of colours that some of these names represent, and even in the case of the base colours – such as *ao-iro, suō* or *murasaki* – it is impossible to reconstruct with any certainty exactly what shade they originally signified. On extremely formal occasions women often wore as many as five layers of these lined robes (*kasaneuchigi*), each with its own lining. Another meaning of the word *kasane*, then, is the combination produced by a whole series of layers that had sleeves of slightly differing lengths. It is this kind of combination which is the object of some criticism on p. 65. It would also seem from the descriptions in this diary that women were in the habit of adding false hems or cuffs on to the sleeves of their mantles and even their jackets in order to accentuate the main point of appreciation.

## WOMEN'S TITLES

Most reference books, both Japanese and English, reproduce the definitions and regulations as laid down in the Yōrō Code of 718, but by Murasaki's time much of this had lost its relevance, so that these lists are only of limited use when trying to reconstruct the system as it operated in the eleventh century; details must come from a study of contemporary historical and literary sources.[2] The most important thing to keep in mind when reading the diary is that there are two distinct groups of women involved. In the Palace the dominant administrative unit for serving the Emperor for his personal needs was the Handmaid's Office (*Naishi no tsukasa*), a sub-office of the Women's Quarters (*Kōkyū*), with a full complement of attendants and maids. But as the importance of empresses and consorts increased in direct relation to the waxing of Fujiwara power, private households began to rival that of the Emperor. As Empress, Shōshi had a household staffed according to the regulations, but she also had a considerable entourage of women who did not have official court positions and who must have been paid for entirely from Fujiwara resources. Most of the women mentioned by Murasaki are of this type, as she was herself, and she clearly distinguished between the two groups. At one point, indeed, she suggests that she does not even know some of the 'palace women' by sight, let alone by name.

Exact details of these private households are hard to come by and probably differed from family to family, but the following outline may not be far from the mark in the case of Shōshi.

(i) three top posts: Envoy (*senji*), Mistress of the Wardrobe (*mikushige-dono*) and Handmaid (*naishi*)

(ii) ladies-in-waiting (*nyōbō*), usually divided into Attendants (*jijū*) and Maids (*nyokurōdo*)

(iii) servants and menials (*nyōkan*).

Although all these terms stem from official titles, they signify rather different posts in the context of private households. There seems to have been, for example, only one *naishi*, Miya no Naishi, in this private system. All other women with this title in the diary are Palace women seconded to the service of Shōshi. From the description of the return to the Palace, it would seem that a number of posts were held by more

---

**2** For this kind of information see W. H. and H. C. McCullough, trans., *A Tale of Flowering Fortunes* (Stanford: Stanford University Press, 1980), vol. 2, pp. 818–22, and F. Hérail, *Fonctions et fonctionnaires japonais au début du XIe siècle* (Paris: Publications Orientalistes de France, 1977), vol. 2, pp. 172–85, 556–75.

than one woman. Miya no Senji was the Envoy, Lady Dainagon and Lady Saishō may both have been Mistress of the Wardrobe, and Miya no Naishi was a Handmaid. Lady Koshōshō was probably an Attendant, as we can presume was Murasaki herself.

## The Author

Perhaps it is surprising that biographical details of a court lady-in-waiting born in Japan in the latter part of the tenth century are available at all, but this was no ordinary woman. Lady Murasaki is, of course, known as the author of the *Genji monogatari*, a work of fiction which is by common consent one of Japan's greatest gifts to world culture. Nevertheless, sources for an account of her life are still somewhat meagre: the 'diary', a collection of short poems, and a few uncertain references in other historical records of the time. These sources have been thoroughly mined, one might say overmined, by generations of Japanese scholars in the attempt to flesh out the life and personality of this remarkable woman; and as the 'diary' covers only two years of her life, albeit two eventful years, it is the collection of poems to which biographers have constantly turned for help. But poetry collections, whether they are understood to be autobiographical or not, are false friends. Certainly, as we have seen, much Japanese court poetry was occasional in nature, and the habit of giving poems prefaces which explain the circumstances of their composition tends to give them a spurious air of reliability, but such is their conventional nature that any attempt to use them as historical record is fraught with difficulties. The standard Japanese biographies of Murasaki[3] lean too heavily on these poems, which are often put to work in dubious contexts. It is for this reason that we must avoid using the poetry as a biographical tool except *in extremis*. The following account will therefore be of necessity somewhat bald.

3 Imai Gen'e, *Murasaki Shikibu*, Jinbutsu sōsho 131 (Tōkyō: Yoshikawa Kōbunkan, 1966); Shimizu Yoshiko, *Murasaki Shikibu*, Iwanami shinsho 854 (Tōkyō: Iwanami Shoten, 1973).

Given the fact that close relatives were set against each other with monotonous regularity and that matters of rank were sacrosanct, it is only natural that Murasaki herself should feel that she had little in common with those in the higher echelons of the ruling Fujiwara clan, despite the fact that they shared a common ancestry. Her particular branch of the family had been coming down in the world for some time and was now on the very fringes of the establishment, filling posts such as provincial governorships, which gave ample opportunity for financial reward but alienated the holder from the tightly knit world of court and capital. The class is known by the generic term *zuryō*. Frequent visits to the provinces were regarded as onerous duties and indeed as a form of exile.

If Murasaki's family were in no way powerful, it had reason to be proud of its literary lineage. Her great-grandfather Kanesuke (877–933) had been closely associated with Ki no Tsurayuki, the driving force behind the rehabilitation of Japanese native verse that led in 905 to the compilation of the first imperial anthology, the *Kokinshū* ('A Collection of Poems Ancient and Modern'). He himself had fifty-seven poems chosen for various imperial anthologies thereafter. Her grandfather Masatada (910?–62) had also been close to Tsurayuki and had seven poems chosen for the *Gosenshū* ('A Later Collection of Poems', commissioned 951). Her father Tametoki continued the tradition of scholarship, but his main interests were in the Chinese classics and poetry in Chinese, and his chief claim to fame must be his role in the education of his daughter. All three of these men left personal poetry collections.[4]

Tametoki was dogged somewhat by ill luck and never rose very high in the court hierarchy. The first mention we have of him is as a boy in Tentoku 4 (960).3.29 at a poetry contest. From this we may deduce that he was born around 945. Soon after 960 he must have graduated as Master of Confucianism (*Monjōshō*), and the first part of

---

4 Tametoki had four poems included in imperial anthologies (*Goshūishū* poems 147, 639, 835 and *Shinkokinshū* poem 1499), one Chinese preface and thirteen Chinese poems in *Honchō reisō*, five Chinese poems in *Ruiju kudaishō*, and one Chinese poem in *Shinsen rōeishū*.

his career seems to have been smooth. He became Junior Secretary Elect of Harima in 968 and served under Emperor Kazan, becoming Sixth Chamberlain and later Senior Secretary in the Ministry of Ceremonial (*Shikibu no Daijō*). This title is part of the origin of Murasaki's name. When Kazan was forced to retire, Tametoki was left out in the cold and remained without an official post for the next ten years. Then in Chōtoku 2 (996).1.7 Emperor Ichijō appointed him Governor of Awaji, a very lowly post indeed. So indignant was he that for once in his life he asserted himself, addressing a memorial to the Emperor which included the lines: 'Bitter study on winter nights brought blood-red tears to soak my sleeves; but in the spring morning on Appointments Day my hopes were high in the blue heavens.' It appears that Ichijō may have been moved by the appeal, because Tametoki was given the more prestigious province of Echizen, whence he took Murasaki in 996.

All that is known about Tametoki's stay in Echizen comes from a preface to one of his poems to be found in the collection *Honchō reisō*, which states that he met some of the seventy Chinese refugees who had landed in Wakasa the previous year and that he exchanged poems with them.

He returned to the capital around Chōhō 2 (1000), and was again without official post for some nine years. There are records of him taking part in numerous poetry competitions, however, so he was not entirely without friends nor entirely destitute. Then in Kankō 8 (1011).2.1 he was appointed Governor of Echigo. This time he took with him his son Nobunori, who fell ill and died there soon after his arrival. Suddenly in Chōwa 3 (1014).6.17 Tametoki abandoned his post and returned to the capital. Two years later in Chōwa 5 (1016).4.29 he retired to the temple at Miidera, where his third son, Jōsen, was a priest. His final rank was Senior Fifth Rank, Upper Grade. The last record we have is dated Kannin 2 (1018).1.21, where he is listed as being present at a banquet held by Regent Yorimichi; he must have died soon after, perhaps in 1020.

When was Murasaki herself born? This is a subject of lively debate, but 973 is generally accepted as being close to the mark. Our knowledge of her early years is extremely sketchy. The prefaces to poems

20–28 and 81–83 in the collection of her poetry suggest strongly that she accompanied her father to Echizen in the summer of 996, and she seems to have returned in 998 to marry Fujiwara no Nobutaka (950?–1001). Nobutaka was almost as old as her father and had a number of other wives – the mid-fourteenth-century genealogy *Sonpi bunmyaku* lists three women who bore him sons. He was in a somewhat similar position to her father and they had worked together under Emperor Kazan, but he had done rather better than Tametoki. From a passage in Sei Shōnagon's *Makura no sōshi* ('Pillow Book')[5] we know him to have been a flamboyant character, and a document dated Chōhō 1 (999).8.27 tells of serious disturbances caused by his high-handed methods as a provincial governor. Tradition has it that his marriage to Murasaki was a happy one; they had a daughter in 999, but he was carried away by an epidemic in Chōhō 3 (1001).4.25.

For the next four or five years Murasaki seems to have led a lonely widow's existence, during which time she began the work of fiction that was to bring her fame and secure her a place at court. We do not know for sure but can assume that she began writing the *Genji monogatari* sometime in either 1002 or 1003, and had written a fair amount by the time she entered the service of Shōshi. It may well be that chapters were read at court and came to the notice of Michinaga, who decided that she would be an excellent addition to his daughter's already impressive entourage.

When Murasaki actually arrived at court is not known. We know from her diary that she entered on 'the twenty-ninth of the twelfth month' (p. 44), but we do not know whether this refers to 1005 or 1006. Much of the evidence is circumstantial, but on Kankō 3 (1006).12.29 Fujiwara no Tokitaka, brother of her deceased husband Nobutaka, was allowed back into court after some misdemeanour, and on Kankō 4 (1007).1.13 her own brother Nobunori was promoted to Sixth Chamberlain. Michinaga may have been rewarding Murasaki on

---

5 See I. Morris, *The Pillow Book of Sei Shōnagon* (London: Oxford University Press, 1967), vol. 1, pp. 124–5. This passage has been omitted from the shortened 1971 Penguin version.

entry into service. This and some matters of internal consistency within the diary suggest that 1006 is the correct date.

It would seem from the diary that Murasaki had few specific duties to perform and acted as cultural companion-cum-tutor to Shōshi. Certainly she had time to record what was going on in some detail and could sit aside from those more active participants in various ceremonies as a kind of observer. It is possible that Michinaga asked her to record the events that constituted his finest hour – the birth of Atsuhira – although it could equally well be argued that women in her position were in the habit of recording such events anyway: the *Eiga monogatari* ('A Tale of Flowering Fortunes'), an extended narrative covering the years 889–1028 and probably compiled by a court lady called Akazome Emon, would seem to be a patchwork quilt of such records. Murasaki seems not to have had an official court post, but was privately employed by Michinaga to serve his daughter. As we have already mentioned, her real name is unknown.

The best information we have about Murasaki's life at court is, of course, the diary, although there are considerable gaps in what she is prepared to reveal. *Sonpi bunmyaku* states flatly that she was Michinaga's concubine, but there is no evidence whatsoever to support this. By her own admission she seems to have been somewhat retiring and even severe. Any *joie de vivre* is carefully balanced by a pervasive melancholy. Perhaps this is one of the reasons her contemporaries never ranked her poetry very highly. Poetry was a social activity, and the reason why she does not appear in a number of important poetry competitions where one might expect to see her name may simply be that she did not wish to participate. There is also a remarkable lack of any record of correspondence or exchange of poems between her and any of her major female contemporaries. Sei Shōnagon had already dropped out of court circles with the death of Teishi in 1000, and we have no way of knowing whether she was alive at this point or not, but Akazome Emon certainly was around; she had been in the service of Rinshi, Michinaga's main wife, for some considerable time. Izumi Shikibu, too, joined Shōshi's entourage in the spring of 1009, but Murasaki's reference to her in the diary suggests a very distant relationship indeed.

As in most cases of women writers and poets of this time, her later years are clouded in uncertainty. Emperor Ichijō died on Kankō 8 (1011).6.22. On the sixteenth of the tenth month of that same year Shōshi moved into the Biwa mansion, and Murasaki presumably went with her. The main clues as to when she might have died are as follows:

(i) As mentioned above, Tametoki suddenly returned to the capital in 1014 and retired in 1016. Might this have been because of Murasaki's death? Possibly, but he was in any case in his early seventies.

(ii) In Murasaki's collection of poetry there is an exchange with a woman called Ise no Tayū at the Kiyomizu temple that can be dated with fair certainty to Chōwa 3 (1014).1.20.

(iii) A passage in the *Eiga monogatari* dated 1025 refers to her in connection with her daughter, but it is not clear from this whether she is alive or not.

(iv) She is not listed among the ladies-in-waiting who accompanied Shōshi on a pilgrimage to the Sumiyoshi Shrine in Chōgen 4 (1031).

(v) This evidence concerns her relationship with Fujiwara no Sanesuke, author of the diary *Shōyūki* and a constant critic of Michinaga. An entry in the *Shōyūki* for Chōwa 2 (1013).5.25 reads:

Yesterday evening when I left Sukehira I sent him in person to the Dowager Empress, telling him to inform her that I would be unable to attend for the time being while the Crown Prince was ill. This morning he returned to say that he had met the lady-in-waiting – the daughter of Tametoki, Governor of Echigo, whom I have often used as an intermediary for various matters in the past – who said that the Crown Prince's illness was not serious, but that he could not attend normal palace business as he still had a fever. Michinaga also felt under the weather, she added.

There are a series of entries of a similar nature in the *Shōyūki* during 1013 and, although they do not mention Murasaki by name, the phrase 'met the lady-in-waiting' appears in many of them. The same is true of a later entry dated Kannin 3 (1019).1.5.

The end result of all this is inconclusive. Murasaki may have died early in 1014 or she may possibly have continued serving Shōshi until as late as 1025. The maturity of vision in the latter part of the *Genji monogatari* suggests the later date, but in the absence of any more information this must remain mere speculation.

Before we leave Murasaki, there are two other members of her family who deserve notice, her brother and her daughter. Her brother Nobunori, generally thought to be her younger brother, is first referred to as a scribe in Kankō 1 (1004).1.11. In Kankō 4 (1007).1.13, as we have seen, he was promoted to Sixth Chamberlain, but he seems to have been rather forgetful and not in the least interested in advancing himself. Apart from the few entries in Murasaki's diary that refer to his lack of intelligence, we have two descriptions of his behaviour. The first is dated Kankō 5 (1008).7.17 and is from an anonymous record in the Imperial Library known as *Fuchiki*, other sections of which can be found translated in Appendix 2.

A letter from the Palace. The messenger was Sixth Chamberlain and Secretary at the Ministry of War Fujiwara no Nobunori. He was given a seat in the first bay of the southern gallery of the main building. Four or five nobles pressed drink on him and he became quite tipsy. He was given a reply for the Emperor and then some gifts . . . He took them in his hand and, still sitting, gave a little nod of the head. Only once! Then he got up, went down into the garden, bowed once more and left.

The second is from Sanesuke's diary and is dated Kankō 5 (1008).12.15.

The priest at the early morning service was given a silver cane and some cotton as a gift. Fifth Chamberlain Hironari and Chamberlains Nobunori and Nobutō carried out a chest full of cotton and divided it into portions just where the priest was standing. Nobunori and Nobutō were the ones who actually carried the chest . . . then Nobunori went down on to the veranda, took the chest with the gifts of cotton for the acolytes in it, and started handing it out. He should have divided it equally among them but instead gave a whole pile of cotton to one man. The other priests started grabbing and there was absolute uproar. Chamberlains seem to have forgotten the rules of late. Every noble present was shocked.

Perhaps as a result of such actions, Nobunori took the opportunity to go to Echigo with his father in 1011 but in any case died soon after his arrival. He seems to have had a fair reputation as a poet, leaving a personal collection and having ten poems chosen for imperial anthologies. His early death in Echigo and a possible relationship with Lady Chūjō, lady-in-waiting to the Priestess of the Kamo Shrines (alluded to in the preface to Poem 764 of the *Gosenshū*), are the subject of stories in a number of tale collections, but this was clearly not the kind of fame for which his elder sister had been hoping.

Murasaki's daughter Kenshi (999–?), on the other hand, more than made up for this disappointment, becoming the object of attention for a number of high-ranking men. In 1025 at the age of twenty-six she became wet nurse to the future Emperor Goreizei. Wet nurses traditionally had great power and it was a coveted position. She then married Takashina no Nariakira and produced a son in 1038. In 1045 she was raised to Junior Third Rank and was made Principal Handmaid (*Naishi no kami*). Still alive in 1078, she may have lived until she was 84. Known as Echigo no Ben and later as Daini no Sanmi, she had thirty-seven poems chosen for imperial anthologies and has left her own collection.

## The Diary

### STRUCTURE

The work now known as the *Murasaki Shikibu nikki* ('Diary of Lady Murasaki') is a rather mixed bag, so the term 'diary' in the title should be taken as a convenient label rather than a definition. It is not a series of day-to-day entries in a journal, although it may have originated as such. Certainly the tradition of recording events for posterity was well established. Men, writing in Sino-Japanese, produced a series of such records ranging from banal everyday information about the weather and official life to more interesting and pungent comments on affairs of state. Women also produced detailed records of the events with which they were most involved, poetry and other competitions, and chronicled the progress of their domestic life, their frequently unhappy love affairs and, in the case of Lady Murasaki, the auspicious birth of a son to the Empress. Much of this diary seems to have been written (or re-written) in retrospect, however. It covers events, ceremonies and memorable scenes at the Japanese court over a two-year period (1008–10), but it also contains passages of intense personal reflection and critical analysis of life at court. It is not as consistently autobiographical as the *Kagerō nikki* ('Gossamer Years'), nor is it as fictionally oriented as the *Izumi Shikibu nikki* ('Diary of Izumi Shikibu'). Indeed, it has more often been compared to Sei Shōnagon's *Makura no sōshi* ('Pillow Book'), with which it shares a love of description and anecdote together with a willingness to criticize fellow ladies-in-waiting. But the *Pillow Book* is also a guidebook to Heian sensibilities, and although Murasaki's diary certainly partakes of the same preconceptions, its aims are very different. It is a highly idiosyncratic mixture of detailed description and penetrating self-analysis, and presents us with its own peculiar problems of interpretation which stem ultimately from the question of its structure. Is it complete? How does it fit together? Is it more than a random collection of observations and if so then for whom was it written?

Figure 1 shows the structure in diagrammatic form:

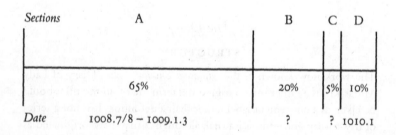

| Sections | A | B | C | D |
|---|---|---|---|---|
| | 65% | 20% | 5% | 10% |
| Date | 1008.7/8 – 1009.1.3 | ? | ? | 1010.1 |

Figure 1

The diary opens with a description of the beauty of the Tsuchimikado mansion in autumn. The year is Kankō 5 (1008). Empress Shōshi became pregnant early in the year and was moved away from the Ichijō Palace and into the mansion on the thirteenth day of the fourth month (21 May). Michinaga arranged for the whole panoply of Buddhist rituals to be set in train, including a grand reading of the *Lotus Sūtra* in thirty sessions, which began on the twenty-third (31 May). Shōshi went back to the Ichijō Palace on the fourteenth day of the sixth month (20 July), only to return to the mansion once again on the sixteenth of the seventh month (20 August). The Tsuchimikado mansion was Michinaga's main residence and belonged, as we have seen, to Shōshi's mother, Rinshi. The withdrawal from the Palace is not just because she will be with her mother; the main reason is that the Palace must be kept clear of any pollution. As Shōshi had been a consort for nine years and was already twenty-one, the pregnancy had been a long time coming. The birth will be the most important moment in Michinaga's career so far, for it means that he will now have the potential to become grandfather to the next Emperor. Murasaki herself, however, ignores the wider political and historical context and we are immediately cast into a world with which familiarity is assumed. Not that Murasaki is unaware of this context; but it is common knowledge – perhaps one of the main reasons for her record – and so goes unsaid. We, of course, need commentary to make sense of much that follows.

The first section begins with a general description, moves on to introduce Her Majesty, and then, in a pattern that we shall find repeated throughout, turns to self-analysis. The narrative proceeds via a series of vignettes, the order of which is far from random. We are introduced to the main figures in correct order of their importance for the ensuing narrative, as well as being given a feel for the atmosphere of court life. Amid awe-inspiring Buddhist ceremonies and the noise and confusion that surrounds the birth itself, we also see scenes that stress the quiet, unhurried nature of life in more normal situations. Michinaga is introduced early on, shown testing Murasaki's own wit. Attention is drawn to the fugitive nature of memory.

There follows a careful transition to a chronologically ordered description of the preparations for the birth of the Prince, which commenced on the ninth of the ninth month and was eventually completed on the morning of the eleventh (13 October). The passages dealing with the birth itself and the whole series of ceremonial events that ensued constitute the bulk of the record. But one of the things that makes this diary of unusual interest is the way that formal descriptions are interspersed with passages of self-analysis which always stem quite naturally from their contexts: in this sense the public and private domains are perfectly interwoven. The concern with detail is at times reminiscent of male diaries in Sino-Japanese, but the concern with the minutiae of dress and ornament and the occasional glimpse we get of rivalry among the women is something that could only have come from a female perspective.

At the end of this main record, about seven tenths through the work, we have a second transition to a more concentrated analysis of Murasaki's own immediate circle. The last dateable event is on Kankō 6 (1009).1.3, and then we shift imperceptibly into a discussion of her fellow ladies-in-waiting, from the point of view first of their looks and then of their characters. This is followed by criticism of the dullness of Shōshi's entourage in general, the timidity of the Empress, and the spinelessness of present-day courtiers, all of which is set in train by the chance sight of a letter in which she and her colleagues are set to ridicule. Then we have tart descriptions of Izumi Shikibu, Akazome Emon and Sei Shōnagon, which lead in turn to further self-analysis. The whole of this section is marked by a strong awareness of a specific addressee through the ubiquitous presence of the auxiliary verb *haberi*, and it ends with what seems to be the finishing touches to a private letter.

At this point we are faced with a complete break. There follow three separate vignettes which have proved strongly resistant to dating. The first is an illustration of Murasaki's wit and learning; the others are poetic dialogues more in the style of the *utamonogatari* tradition, where context and poem follow each other in intricate procession. The last tenth of the work sees a return to the record style, but it deals with only a few events in the first month of Kankō 7 (1010). There is therefore a large gap between the early record and this last description, a gap in which, among other things, a second prince, Atsunaga, has been born. Then the account simply breaks off, not exactly in mid sentence but not at any clearly defined point either.

As may be expected, such a strange arrangement has given rise to numerous theories as to the genesis of the work, many of which are mutually contradictory but equally possible. The first thing to be examined, however, is the evidence from other sources that the diary we have today may well be incomplete.

## EVIDENCE OF EXTRA FRAGMENTS

### (a) The 'Nikkiuta' appendix

Murasaki's collection of short poems exists in a number of different manuscripts, which scholars have analysed into two main groups, known as the 'Old Recensions' and the 'Teika Recensions'. Appended to three extant copies of the 'Old Recensions' group is a set of seventeen poems collected under the subtitle 'Nikkiuta' or 'Poems from the diary'. It is thought that these poems were probably collected by the scholar Fujiwara no Teika (1162–1241) on finding that the 'Old Recensions' texts in his possession omitted many of the poems to be found in the diary. The problem here, however, is that the first five poems in this appendix do not in fact appear in the diary as we have it today. Their content and prefaces are such that they can be dated with fair certainty to Kankō 5 (1008).5.5–6, which strongly suggests that the person who compiled the appendix had in his or her possession a diary that was larger than the one we have today. Note that if this is the case, this passage would predate the present beginning sections, which must refer to autumn 1008.

### (b) The Eiga monogatari ('A Tale of Flowering Fortunes')

It is well known that Murasaki's diary was used extensively as a source by the compiler of the *Eiga monogatari*, to the extent that whole passages were sometimes simply lifted piecemeal.[6] This borrowing is usually held to start with the very beginning of the diary – autumn at the Tsuchimikado mansion – but some of the prefaces to the five poems mentioned above also bear a striking resemblance to that part of the *Eiga monogatari* that immediately precedes the description of autumn

6 See W. H. and H. C. McCullough, op. cit., vol. 1, pp. 53–63.

and which deals with the readings of the *Lotus Sūtra* that started on Kankō 5.5.5.[7]

### (c) Reconstruction

A comparison of these texts reveals the following fragment:

At the Tsuchimikado mansion the fifth scroll of the thirty readings of the Lotus Sūtra was read out on the fifth of the fifth month. It was the Devadatta chapter, which gave me to imagine that the Buddha had picked fruit not so much for Devadatta as for His Excellency himself today.

> Ah marvellous!
> Today is the fifth of the fifth they say;
> Eminently fitting for the fifth scroll of the Law.

They must have taken special pains to prepare the offering branches.
[The *Eiga monogatari* has a full description of the ceremonies on this occasion, but there is no other text with which comparisons can be made. Similarities resume with the following:]
That evening Her Majesty was again present at the Hall of Dedication, where she must have spoken with her sister Kenshi. Right below us the lake looked even clearer than during the day, lit as it was by a combination of flares and ceremonial torches, and I could smell the fresh scent of sweet flags. Although I had much on my mind, I fought back my tears, thinking as I did so of how interesting it all ought to have seemed.

> In the waters of the lake that reflect the brightness of the flares
> Dwells the light of the Law that will be clear for ever.

Although I was evasively composing poems about the ceremony, Lady Dainagon sitting opposite me looked most distressed, belying both her age and her good looks.

> The flares that light the clear lake to the depths
> Are so dazzling, they put my own sad self to shame.

7 ibid., p. 267.

The ladies-in-waiting returned to their rooms at dawn, walking down the corridors, over the bridge, along the veranda of the west wing and through the main building. As they passed in front of Her Excellency's apartments, where sūtras were being recited, many of them must have been awe-struck by the sheer magnificence of the mansion; even those women who when on private pilgrimages usually try to convince themselves, if not others, of their own worth by surrounding themselves with attendants and who insist on having the way cleared for them with such an air of self-importance.

Day was just dawning as I went out on to the bridge and leaned on the balustrade, watching the water flow from beneath the rooms in the back corridor. The sky was no less beautiful than when filled with spring haze or autumn mist. I knocked at the corner shutters of Lady Koshōshō's room. She opened both halves, top and bottom, and came out on to the veranda. As we both sat there looking out over the garden, I composed:

> Now I see my face floating there
> My sad tears mingle with the stream
> To make a waterfall of complaint.

To which she replied:

> One alone fighting back the tears;
> In the face of the water
> Whose is the other face sadly floating there?

Together we spent the night gazing out, finally going inside only when dawn arrived. Wrapping up a long root, she gave it to me with the following:

> Sweet flags afloat
> In the sad and muddy waters of this mundane world –
> What of this root and what of my tearful voice today?

My reply was:

> What it is I cannot fathom.
> Today too this sleeve of mine
> Can neither hold this root or stem my tears.

The above fragment constitutes very strong evidence that the compiler of the *Eiga monogatari* had more than the present diary at her disposal. The reason why more of it does not actually appear in the *Eiga monogatari* is that the compiler made a conscious attempt to cut out all the more personal aspects of Murasaki's account, and much of this fragment consists of precisely that. It would also seem highly likely that the compiler of the 'Nikkiuta' appendix, probably Teika himself, had this larger diary in his possession. Extra evidence for this is supplied by a passage in Teika's diary, the *Meigetsuki*, for Tenpuku 1 (1233).3.20. This entry records that a picture scroll consisting of paintings and poems illustrating the twelve months of the year (*tsukinami-e*), originally a gift to Teika's daughter from Princess Shikishi, is now to be given to the reigning Empress. The poem for the fifth month was recorded as 'Diary of Murasaki Shikibu: a dawn scene'. As no such poem appears in the diary that we have today, this must be one of the poems above, probably 'Now I see my face floating there'.

## DATE OF COMPOSITION

What if we accept the above hypothesis that the diary as we have it is incomplete? As the extra fragments identified above predate the present beginning of the diary, it follows that the beginning must be considered lost. The only reason that a large number of scholars continue to argue against this idea is the fact that the present beginning constitutes such a superb introductory passage, so fitting indeed that it is hard to believe that anything could have preceded it. In this case, the only way we can explain away the existence of the Kankō 5.5.5 passage is to posit either an *Ur*-diary, out of which the present one was presumably extracted and rewritten, or to posit another separate diary. But this is all entirely supposition, based on a certain 'feeling' about the inviolability of the beginning as we have it now. One sympathizes, but as yet no one has come up with a satisfactory argument for denying the theory that the beginning of the diary has been lost. It may, of course, be that much more has in fact been lost, but there is no way of knowing.

What of Section B? In contrast to Section A, which is usually known as the 'record' part, Section B has traditionally been given the name 'letter' part (*shōsokubumi*). Why this is so should be clear from the last passages of this section, where it is obvious that there is a specific addressee in mind. Obvious, that is, unless you consider that this may actually be a narrative technique, a fictional letter. There is also the ubiquitous presence of the polite auxiliary verb *haberi*, which has the effect of stressing the existence of a receiver. Indeed for some time Section B was considered to be a real intruder, a letter that had been interpolated into the diary by mistake. This is an attractive idea at first sight but cannot be accepted as a feasible explanation, for one main reason: the smoothness with which A runs into B. The transition from record to personal comment takes place gradually over a number of paragraphs. If we insist on seeing B as an interpolation, then we are driven to the somewhat unsatisfactory conclusion that a second hand deliberately rewrote the beginning of the letter so that the join would be invisible.

While the smoothness of the join is undeniable, there still remain a number of elements that suggest that Sections A and B are by no means an organic unit. In the first place, the contrast in content and style is striking, and the presence of the occasional personal comment and passage of self-analysis in Section A does nothing to dispel such an impression. In the second place, there is a marked imbalance in the frequency of the auxiliary verb *haberi*. In Section B *haberi* appears 136 times, acting in its normal role as an auxiliary expressing politeness to the person being addressed, quite in character for a letter being written to someone specific. It also appears, however, in Section A, where one would not normally expect it to be present at all. Admittedly, it only occurs here twenty-five times and then subject to special constraints, but its very presence is an anomaly and demands an explanation. *Haberi* does not, it will be noted, appear in the extra fragment nor in Section C. The fact that it reappears six times in Section D, which is also 'record', suggests that A and D may have something in common. An analysis of its usage in Section A shows that it probably marks passages that were added later: these are highlighted in the translation by the addition of a phrase such as 'I remember that . . .' This raises the possibility that A was to some extent rewritten to fit B. But when did this occur? And why was the revision felt to be necessary?

It is useful to remind ourselves of when the various sections were written. Section A covers events from autumn Kankō 5 (1008) to Kankō 6 (1009).1.3. There are also some internal clues. Fujiwara no Kintō is described as a Major Counsellor (p. 19) and Fujiwara no Yukinari is given the title Middle Counsellor (p. 37). Both of these men were appointed to these positions (elect) in Kankō 6 (1009).3.4, so this must have been written, or rewritten, after that date. We know too that Prince Nakatsukasa died in Kankō 6 (1009).7.28, and as Murasaki talks about him as if he were still alive, it is reasonable to assume that Section A was written in the late spring or early summer of 1009.

Section B contains no dateable material as such, of course, but Fujiwara no Tadanobu is called Major Counsellor, which places it again as post-Kankō 6 (1009).3.4, and Akazome Emon's husband is called the Governor of Tanba, which places it even later, post-Kankō 7 (1010).3.30. Unless this itself is a later amendment, B must have been written after this date, which means that a considerable distance separates the writing of A and B, evidence which tends to conflict with the smoothness with which they are joined.

Section C cannot be dated with any certainty, but it is thought these vignettes may refer to events in Kankō 6 (1009).9.11.

Section D deals with events from Kankō 7 (1010).1.1 to 1.15. One can assume that they were written soon after the events themselves, although the use of *haberi* also suggests some degree of rewriting.

Based on the above, the following picture emerges:

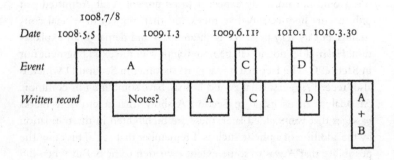

Figure 2

Section A was written some four or five months after the event it describes, possibly based on notes taken at the time. This would have been a woman's court diary that combined detailed description with the occasional passage of personal reflection – very much the kind of record that Akazome Emon must have relied on heavily for much of the *Eiga monogatari*. It may have been a formal diary produced at the behest of Michinaga, but the personal material makes this a little doubtful. Sections C and D were written on or soon after the events they refer to. Then, sometime after 1010.3.30, Murasaki herself picked up Section A and carried on writing where she had left off. The continuation was in a far more personal vein and was designed to be sent to someone specific. Deciding to send A with B, she not only ensured they flowed on smoothly but also cast her eye back over A, adding in the process a number of personal and explanatory remarks. The use of *haberi* betrays, as it were, the presence of these later additions. The same applies to D, but C reveals no sign of rewriting and so may indeed be an errant fragment.

We do not know why Section A stops where it does. There are various theories, but none are conclusive. And to whom was Murasaki writing when she finished Section B? It is sometimes argued that we are dealing with a fictional letter here, or even with an 'open letter', but we have no proof either way. If it were addressed to another lady-in-waiting, then she must have been absent from court for some time. Numerous other possibilities have been suggested, but none is more likely than Murasaki's own daughter Kenshi. One might object that Kenshi would have been too young to have been interested in such information, but then Shōshi herself became Imperial Consort at the age of eleven. Certainly this would explain the proprietary tone of much of Section B where Murasaki does seem to be trying to teach by example.

Lastly, did Murasaki intend the diary to be exactly as we have it today? From the evidence adduced above this would appear highly unlikely. It is probable that the reconstructed fragment has become detached from the beginning, but anything else must remain mere speculation. Whether Sections A, C and D were originally parts of a much longer record that Murasaki kept is impossible to say.

## THE NATURE OF THE WORK

Given that we are dealing with such a fragmented text, part public part private record, how are we to approach it? Is it in fact anything more than a collection of jottings, notes and observations that would hardly merit attention were it not for the fame of its author?

Of course the fact that it was written by the author of the *Genji monogatari* is of major importance, but the work is also significant in that it helps us to explain the emergence of such a magnificent fiction. Up to this point Japanese prose had consisted largely of stories of the 'fairy tale' type and women's autobiographical writing. The most important example of the latter was the *Gossamer Years*, a claustrophobic chronicle of frustrated passion and listless days. Murasaki's diary exhibits a further stage in the rapid development of Japanese. We have already suggested that the record we see in the diary may have been done almost as a kind of exercise.

In the context of record-taking, the recitation of detail and fact becomes its own justification. The problem with detail, however, is that it often hides rather than reveals the significance of what is being described. What, for example, is Murasaki's attitude to this display of Fujiwara power? Knowing her acute awareness of the realities and psychological ramifications of power as demonstrated in the *Genji monogatari*, it is extremely difficult to believe that she simply acquiesced in what she saw. There is the occasional moment in the diary when one feels a hesitation, but usually the moment is personalized and the vision returns to her own predicament; there is little overt sign that she saw the status quo as anything but immutable. It is tempting to deduce that she simply was not in a position to do anything but praise Fujiwara power and elegance. The cavalier way that the Emperor is treated, for example, is seen to be simply how things are.

But can one look a little further? Was she not aware of the tendency of such records to become opaque and is this why the text has a tendency to slip into personal anecdote and self-analysis given half the chance? The very opaqueness might then be seen as betraying an underlying sense of resistance.

The other interesting element here is the confessionalism that emerges here and there in the 'record' section and then fully near the end of the 'letter'. It is this willingness to subject the self to analysis that gives Heian women's writing much of its psychological maturity and penetration. It may not have been a modern self that was discovered and opened up to the world, but it was a self. It is often assumed that because Buddhism brands the self as a pernicious illusion a sense of self could never really develop, but the opposite might well be argued: namely that such emphasis had to be placed on this denial precisely because the concept was very much alive. And, although the ties between confession and salvation cannot be said to be as strong as in the case of Christianity, the connection was nevertheless made. Priests and nuns made vows; attachment to this world was certainly a sin that should be atoned for. There was also the possibility of personal salvation through belief in Amitābha Buddha. The specific nature of Buddhist beliefs among the women courtiers at this time had a very strong influence on the development of writing in the confessional mode.

One of the central concerns of the diary, by its very form, is the nature of time. In most works by women prior to this diary, time was organized on a personal basis, a process that refers not to the outer world of society with its dates and ceremonies, and not even to the way one year follows the next, but rather inward to inner rhythms and perceptions. Murasaki's diary contains both types of time. As a figure in the public arena recording a series of ceremonies, she is subject to external time not only physically but also in the sense that the diary is organized according to such principles. As a person, she is governed by internal time and, above all, by memory. Given these two conflicting kinds of time and the two conflicting worlds of self and society, Murasaki proves remarkably successful in combining them, and the result is an unrivalled presentation of Heian court life from outside and from within by someone who is at once participant and observer. In another sense the diary can be understood to be 'about' the workings of memory, about the effect that time and mind have on events. As description slides into reminiscence, we are made aware of how reconstruction of an event must rely on an ever so fallible memory.

'How is it that a little incident like this suddenly comes back to one, whereas something that moved one deeply at the time can simply be forgotten with the passage of the years?' she remarks at the end of one passage near the beginning. This is perhaps the key: the process of remembering and forgetting is itself an eternal fascination, and the diary is to be an illustration of that process. This best explains those sections where she goes out of her way to tell us that she was not actually present, or did not have a very good vantage point, or where she employs verb forms that suggest varying degrees of uncertainty. Sheer detail is a major device for re-creating a past event, but here it goes hand-in-hand with constant little reminders of how very difficult such a task can be.

# THE DIARY OF
# LADY MURASAKI

As autumn advances, the Tsuchimikado mansion looks unutterably beautiful. Every branch on every tree by the lake and each tuft of grass on the banks of the stream takes on its own particular colour, which is then intensified by the evening light. The voices in ceaseless recitation of sūtras are all the more impressive as they continue throughout the night; in the slowly cooling breeze it is difficult to distinguish them from the endless murmur of the stream.

Her Majesty listens to her ladies-in-waiting engaged in idle gossip. She must be in some distress, but manages to hide her feelings as if nothing were amiss; perhaps this calls for no comment, and yet it is quite extraordinary how she can cause a change of heart in someone so disenchanted with life as myself and make me quite forget my troubles – if only I had sought solace for my unhappiness by taking service with her much earlier.

It is still the depth of night. The moon has clouded over, darkening the shadows under the trees. There come voices: 'Can we open the shutters?' 'But the servants will not be ready yet!' 'Attendant! Open up!' Then the bell for the dawn watch suddenly wakes everyone up and the Ritual of the Five Great Mystic Kings begins.[1] The voice of

1 The ritual took place in the east wing of the mansion and involved a row of five altars behind each of which was placed a statue of one of the five great deities (*Vidyārāja*): Fudō (*Acalanātha*), Gōzanze (*Trailokyavijaya*), Gundari Yasha (*Kuṇḍalī*), Daiitoku (*Yamāntaka*) and Kongō Yasha (*Vajrayakṣa*), who symbolized the wrathful energies of the Five Buddhas of Esoteric Buddhism. In this case the object of the ritual is to pray for a safe birth and to bless certain objects that belonged to the mother-to-be. See ground-plan 2 (Appendix 1).

3

each priest as he tries to best his neighbour can be heard near and far, solemn and awe-inspiring. Then, the ritual over, the Archbishop of the Kannon'in leads twenty acolytes in procession from the east wing over to the main building to cast magic spells; as they cross the bridge, their thundering feet sound strange and unfamiliar. When the Abbot of the Hosshōji and the Bishop of the Jōdoji return to their lodgings in the stable lodge and the library, both accompanied by retinues dressed in priestly robes, I follow them in my mind's eye as they pass over the magnificent Chinese bridges and disappear into the trees. Preceptor Saigi remains prostrate before the statue of Daiitoku deep in prayer.

As the maids and servants all assemble, dawn breaks.

I look out from my room at the head of the corridor into the light morning mist.[2] Dew is still on the ground, but His Excellency is already out in the garden ordering his attendants to clear the stream of some obstruction. Plucking a sprig from a large cluster of maiden-flowers that blooms there on the south side of the bridge, he peers in over the top of the curtain frame. The sight of him, so magnificent, makes me conscious of my own dishevelled appearance, and so when he presses me for a poem, I use it as an excuse to move to where my inkstone is kept:

> Now I see the colour of this maiden-flower in bloom,
> I know how much the dew discriminates against me.

'Quick, aren't we!' says he with a smile and asks for my brush:

> It is not the dew that chooses where to fall:
> Does not the flower choose the colour that it desires?[3]

2 See ground-plan 2 (Appendix 1). Murasaki's room was probably in the back corridor or gallery that ran between the main building and the east wing. These galleries were often partitioned with sliding screens, panels and curtains about four feet high so as to form small rooms. Not much privacy could be expected with such an arrangement.
3 A typical exchange of short poems with a premium placed on wit and the ability to improvise. It is common to find personal feelings expressed by oblique reference to objects in this way. His Excellency's reply thereby manages to be equivocal: is there blame or praise here?

One quiet evening as Lady Saishō and I are talking together, His Excellency's eldest son pulls up the bottom of the blind and seats himself down. He is very grown-up for his age and looks most elegant. The earnestness with which he talks of love – 'Ah women! Such difficult creatures at times!' – it gives the lie to those who dismiss him as a callow youth; I find him rather unsettling. We are still talking in generalities when suddenly he is off, murmuring something about there being 'too many maiden-flowers in the field'; I remember thinking how like the hero of a romance he seemed.[4]

How is it that a little incident like this suddenly comes back to one, whereas something that moved one deeply at the time can simply be forgotten with the passage of the years?

I was absent from the mansion the day the Governor of Harima gave a banquet as a forfeit for losing a game of *go*, and it was only later that I was given the opportunity to see the tray made for the occasion. The Chinese stand was exquisitely fashioned, and at the edge of the water was written:

> Picked up from the Shirara sands of Ki, they say,
> May these pebbles grow to mighty rocks!

The women had the most beautiful fans on that occasion.[5]

4 His Excellency's son Yorimichi is here quoting from a poem by Ono no Yoshiki, which can be found in the first imperial collection, the *Kokinshū* ('A Collection of Poems Ancient and Modern', *c.* 905): *If I tarry in this field so full of maiden-flowers, I am in danger of gaining a bad reputation.* The change of tense in the translation is deliberate, for it is at this point that the descriptions become more specific in time and place. This is also where we encounter the first use of the auxiliary verb *haberi*, which suggests a certain distance in the narration, occurring as it does in passages where Murasaki is clearly commenting on something that she has written, or that has happened, much earlier.

5 Elaborate trays were made, often with miniature land- or seascapes in them, to act as the centrepiece at competitions and banquets. In this case we have a beach scene and the poem has been written on the silver 'water' that represents the sea. The game itself was probably a form of jackstones rather than the modern game of *go*, and the poem plays on the 'stones'. The idea that pebbles would eventually grow into rocks was a common conceit and often linked to felicitations for a long reign. Through its phrasing,

Sometime after the twentieth of the eighth month, those nobles and senior courtiers whose presence was required at the mansion started to stay the night. They would take naps on the bridge and the veranda of the east wing, and play music in desultory fashion until dawn. The younger members, who were as yet unskilled in either *koto* or flute, held competitions to see who was best at chanting sūtras and they practised the latest songs together; it was a perfect match for both place and occasion.

There were also evenings when Tadanobu, Master of Her Majesty's Household, Tsunefusa, Adviser of the Left, Norisada, Commander of the Military Guards, and Junior Captain Narimasa, Governor of Mino, sat and played music together. A formal concert was not held, however, presumably because His Excellency had decided it would have been inappropriate. Those who had left Her Majesty's service some years ago were suddenly reminded of their long absence and crowded back, so with all the bustle and activity we could find not a moment to ourselves.

On the twenty-sixth, the blending of the incense balls was finished and Her Majesty distributed them to her women.[6] Those who had helped prepare them all gathered round. Returning to my room, I looked in at Lady Saishō's door, only to find her asleep. She lay with her head pillowed on a writing box, her face all but hidden by a series of robes – dark red lined with green, purple lined with dark red – over which she had thrown a deep crimson gown of unusually glossy silk. The shape of her forehead was enchanting and so delicate. She looked

---

the poem alludes to another poem produced on a similar but rather more formal occasion that was held some thirty-five years previously in 973. It is this allusion that explains the enigmatic statement about fans that follows, because the record of the 973 event (a record that still remains) specifically refers to the exquisite fans that had been given out as prizes. 'On that occasion' therefore refers to 973 rather than 1008. Murasaki is quietly showing just how erudite she can be, and in the process gives us an example of the way memory can move in unpredictable fashion.

6 Incense was carefully mixed and put into containers, which were then buried in the ground, preferably in a sunny area near water, for a number of days. In this case they were allowed to cure for twelve days and were tested on the ninth of the following month. The testing would take the form of a competition.

just like one of those princesses you find depicted in illustrations. I pulled back the sleeve that covered her face.

'You remind me of a fairy-tale princess!' I said.

She looked up with a start.

'You are dreadful!' she said, propping herself up. 'Waking people up like that without a thought!'

I remember being struck by the attractive way her face suddenly flushed. So it is that someone normally very beautiful can look even more beautiful than ever on occasions.

On the ninth of the ninth month Lady Hyōbu brought me floss-silk damp with chrysanthemum dew.

'Here,' she said. 'Her Excellency sent it especially for you. She said you were to use it carefully to wipe old age away!'

I was about to send it back with the poem:

> Chrysanthemum dew:
> I brush my sleeve to gain a little youth,
> But let she who owns the flower have the thousand years they bring.

But then they told me that Her Excellency had already returned to her apartments; there was no point, I told myself, so let the matter drop.[7]

As night fell, I went to attend Her Majesty. It was a beautiful moon-lit night. Lady Koshōshō, Lady Dainagon and the others were sitting at their respective places near the veranda, the hems of their long trains cascading out from beneath the blinds. The incense was brought in and placed on a burner for Her Majesty to test. We discussed how beautiful the garden was looking and how unreasonably long it was taking for the vines to show their autumn colours, but Her Majesty

---

7 The ninth of the ninth month was the day of the Chrysanthemum Festival. It was believed that to wipe one's face with material that had been left out on chrysanthemums overnight to protect the flowers and soak in the dew would bring rejuvenation. There may be more to this little episode than meets the eye, but if there is ironic intent on the part of Her Excellency and sarcasm in Murasaki's reply, it is difficult to recover with any certainty.

seemed to be in considerable discomfort. When it came time for
the priests to perform their rites, I went in with her feeling most
uneasy.

I was called away and returned to my own room. Intending to rest
for a while, I fell asleep and about midnight I awakened to a scene of
great bustle and noise.

As dawn approached on the morning of the tenth, they changed
all the furnishings and Her Majesty was moved to a white-
curtained dais.[8] His Excellency was in charge, and his sons, together
with other courtiers of fourth and fifth rank, were milling about hanging up curtains and bringing in mats and cushions. It was all extremely
noisy. Her Majesty was very restless all day and clearly in great
distress.

Loud spells were cast in order to transfer evil influences. All the
priests who had been at the mansion for the last few months were
present, of course, but they were now joined by everyone worthy of
the name exorcist who had been ordered down from the major
temples. As they crowded in, you could imagine every Buddha in the
universe flying down to respond. Those famed as Ying-Yang diviners
had also been asked to attend. Surely not a god in the land could have
failed to prick up his ears, I felt.

All day long there were messengers leaving to request the reading of
sūtras; and it continued on throughout the night.

The ladies-in-waiting sent from the Palace were seated in the eastern gallery. To the west of the dais were the women acting as mediums, each surrounded by a pair of screens. Curtains had been hung at
the entrance to each enclosure, where sat an exorcist whose role it was
to intone loud spells. To the south, the archbishops and bishops of
greatest importance sat in rows; it was most impressive to hear their
hoarse voices, now in prayer, now in censure, loud enough, I felt, to

8 See ground-plan 3 (Appendix 1) for the layout at this point. The dais itself was about a
foot high, covered with mats and cushions, and surrounded by a series of curtains hung
from a standing frame. As we find out later on, the usual dais was not dismantled but
simply pushed into another part of the main room.

call up the manifestation of Fudō in living form.[9] When I counted later, there must have been over forty people crammed into that narrow space between the sliding screens to the north and the dais itself. Hardly able to move an inch, they were all in a trance, quite carried away by it all. Unfortunately there was no room for those who had just arrived from home. No one could find the hem of her train or her sleeves in the crush, and the older women, whom one expected to set an example, were beside themselves trying as best they could to hide their tears.

At dawn on the eleventh, two sets of sliding screens on the north side were taken away and Her Majesty was moved into the back gallery.[10] Since it was not possible to hang up blinds, she was surrounded by a series of overlapping curtains. The Archbishop, Bishop Jōjō and the Bishop for General Affairs were in attendance performing rites. Bishop Ingen, having added some portentous phrases to an invocation composed by His Excellency the day before, now read it out slowly in solemn and inspiring tones. It could not have been more impressive, especially when His Excellency himself decided to join in the prayers. Surely nothing could go wrong now, I thought; and yet such was the strain that none of us could hold back her tears. No matter how much we told ourselves how unlucky it might be to cry like this, it was impossible to refrain.

His Excellency, concerned that Her Majesty might feel even worse with so many people crowded around, made everyone move away to the south and east; only those whose presence was considered essential were allowed to remain. Her Excellency, Lady Saishō and Lady Kura were in attendance inside the curtains, as were the Bishop of the Ninnaji and the Palace Priest from the Miidera. His Excellency was

9 One of the five guardian deities mentioned in note 1, Fudō (*Acalanātha* or the Immovable One) was of particularly ferocious mien. He was equipped with a rope in his left hand, a demon-quelling sword in the right, sported two large fangs, and had flames springing from his back.

10 This move was presumably dictated by the soothsayers. There seems to have been no veranda at the back of the building, so this was as far north as Her Majesty could be moved. See ground-plan 3 (Appendix 1).

shouting orders to all and sundry in such a loud voice that the priests were almost drowned out and could hardly be heard. In the remaining section of the back gallery sat Lady Dainagon, Lady Koshōshō, Miya no Naishi, Ben no Naishi, Lady Nakatsukasa, Lady Tayū, and Lady Ōshikibu – His Excellency's envoy, you know.[11] It was only to be expected that they should seem distraught, for they had all been in service for so many years, but even I, who had not known Her Majesty for long, knew instinctively how very grave the situation was.

Another group of women, among them Nakatsukasa, Shōnagon and Koshikibu, who had been wet nurses to His Excellency's second, third and youngest daughters, squeezed their way in front of the curtains that hung as a divider behind us, with the result that people could barely pass along the narrow passage at the rear of the two daises, and those who did manage to push their way through could hardly tell whom they were jostling.

Whenever the men felt like it, they looked over the curtains. Somehow one expected this kind of behaviour from His Excellency's sons, and even from Kanetaka, Adviser of the Right, and Junior Captain Masamichi, but not from the Adviser of the Left or the Master of Her Majesty's Household; they were usually much more circumspect. We lost all sense of shame being seen in such a state, our eyes swollen with weeping. In retrospect it may have been amusing, I suppose, but at the time we must have presented a sorry sight, rice falling on our heads like snow and our clothes all crumpled and creased.[12]

When they started to snip Her Majesty's hair and made her take her vows, everyone was thrown into confusion and wondered what on earth was happening. Then in the midst of all this despair, she was safely delivered. Everyone, priests and laymen alike, who was crowded into that large area stretching all the way from the main room to the

11 This little interjection, using the colloquial particle *yo*, occurs more than once in the diary. It is one of a number of signs that the text is layered: such remarks seem to have been added at a later date, perhaps during the process of copying.
12 The rice is being thrown in the air as part of the rituals to keep all evil influences at bay.

southern gallery and the balustrade, broke once more into chanting and prostrated themselves in prayer until the afterbirth appeared.

The women in the gallery to the east seem to have become mixed up with the senior courtiers with the result that Lady Kochūjō came face to face with First Chamberlain Yorisada. Her embarrassment later became the source of some amused comment. Very elegant and always most particular about her appearance, she had made herself up in the morning, but now her eyes were swollen with weeping and tears had made her powder run here and there; she was a dreadful sight and looked most odd. I remember what a shock I had when I saw how Lady Saishō's face had changed too. And I hate to think of how I must have looked. It was a relief that no one could actually recall how anyone else had looked on that occasion.

At the moment of birth what awful wails of anguish came from the evil spirits! Preceptor Shin'yo had been assigned to Gen no Kurōdo, a priest called Myōso to Hyōe no Kurōdo, and the Master of Discipline from the Hōjūji to Ukon no Kurōdo. Miya no Naishi's enclosure was being overseen by Preceptor Chisan; he was thrown to the ground by the spirits and was in such distress that Preceptor Nengaku had to come to his aid with loud spells. Not that his powers were on the wane, it was just that the evil proved so very persistent. The priest Eikō, brought in to help Lady Saishō's exorcist, became hoarse from shouting spells all night. There was further chaos when not all of the women managed to accept the spirits to whom they had been assigned.[13]

It was already midday, but we all felt just as if the morning sun had risen into a cloudless sky. Our delight on hearing Her Majesty had been safely delivered knew no bounds, and how could we have been anything but ecstatic that it was a boy. Those ladies who yesterday had wilted and this morning had been sunk in a mist of autumn tears all

13 Since at least some of these women have already just been described as serving close by Her Majesty, it is doubtful whether they themselves were acting as mediums. It is more likely that, as high-ranking ladies-in-waiting, each of them was made responsible for an enclosure and that the gruelling work of being a medium had been entrusted to professional substitutes. An exorcist has been assigned to each medium, but in some cases further help was obviously necessary.

took their leave and retired to rest. The older women, who were best fitted for the task, were in attendance on Her Majesty.

Their Excellencies moved through to another part of the mansion to distribute offerings of thanks both to those priests who had carried out rituals and chanted sūtras for months past and to those who had come in response to more recent demands. Gifts were also presented to those doctors and diviners who had shown special skill in their respective arts. I assume that preparations for the ceremony of the first bathing were already proceeding at the Palace.[14]

In the women's apartments servants brought in new dresses in large bundles and packages. Both the embroidery on the jackets and the hem-stitching with mother-of-pearl inlay on the trains had been grossly overdone, and the women tried to hide them from each other, concentrating on their powder and their dresses and fussing about why the fans they had ordered had not yet arrived.

Looking out as usual from my room at the end of the corridor, I noticed the Master of Her Majesty's Household waiting by the side door in the company of Yasuhira, Master of the Crown Prince's Household, and various other nobles. His Excellency emerged and gave orders that the stream be cleared of the leaves that had been blocking it for some days past. Everyone was in high spirits. In the general atmosphere, which must have allowed even those with private worries to forget their troubles for the time being, it was only natural that Tadanobu, as Master of Her Majesty's Household, should find it hard to hide his own particular delight, although he tried not to smile too broadly. Kanetaka was sitting on the veranda of the east wing exchanging jokes with Takaie, Middle Counsellor Elect.

14 These preparations included making the bathtub and other ceremonial objects. Murasaki's assumption here is incorrect. The bathtub was made at the Tsuchimikado mansion rather than at the Palace and the order was not given until the baby had been safely delivered. His Excellency Michinaga's diary has the following entry for this day: 'The boy was safely delivered about noon. Presented gifts to the priests and diviners who had been present, each according to rank. At the same time the child had his first feed, the umbilical cord was cut, and they began to make the bath tub.' The carpenters were given less than six hours to complete the task.

First Chamberlain Yorisada, who had brought the ceremonial sword from the Palace, was charged by his Excellency to return and report the safe birth to the Emperor. That day was the day the imperial messenger left for Ise, so he would not have been allowed to enter the Palace itself, being obliged to report standing outside instead.[15] He received gifts from His Excellency, but I was not present.

The ceremonial cutting of the umbilical cord was done by Her Excellency, and Lady Tachibana performed the first offering of the breast. Lady Ōsaemon was chosen to be the wet nurse since she had been in service for some time and was known and liked by all. She is the daughter of Michitoki, the Governor of Bitchū, and wife of Chamberlain Hironari.

The first bathing took place at about six in the evening, I think.[16] Torches were lit and Her Majesty's servants, wearing white vestments over short green robes, carried in the hot water. The stands that held the tubs were covered in white cloth. Chikamitsu, Chief of the Office of Weaving, and Nakanobu, the Chief Attendant, bore the tubs up to the blinds and passed them in to the two women in charge of the water, Lady Kiyoiko and Harima; they in turn made sure it was only lukewarm. Then two other women, Ōmoku and Muma, filled up sixteen pitchers, emptying what remained straight into the bath tub. They were all wearing gauze mantles, with trains and jackets of taffeta, and had their hair done up most attractively with hairpins and white ribbons. Lady Saishō was in charge of the bathing itself, with Lady Dainagon acting as her assistant. Dressed in unusual aprons, they both looked extremely elegant.

15 A messenger was regularly dispatched on the eleventh of the ninth month from the court to Ise, sacred centre of the Imperial cult. Shintō treated blood as a pollutant. Having been to the Tsuchimikado mansion, Yorisada is now defiled from contact with the birth and cannot enter the Palace for fear of infecting the messenger.
16 Was Murasaki perhaps not present at this and the following ceremonies? Later on, for instance, she is unsure as to who performed the readings. In any case, she was clearly trying to be as careful as possible in what she recorded. For a sense of what is going on at this juncture, see ground-plan 4 (Appendix 1).

His Excellency carried the baby prince in his arms, preceded by Lady Koshōshō with the sword and Miya no Naishi with the tiger's head.[17] Her jacket was decorated with a pine-cone pattern and her train had a wave design woven into it, giving it the appearance of a printed seascape. The waistband was of thin gauze embroidered with a Chinese vine pattern. Lady Koshōshō's train was decorated with autumn grasses, butterflies and birds sketched in glittering silver. We were none of us free to do exactly as we pleased because of the rules about the use of silk, so she had obviously tried something unusual at the waistline.

His Excellency's two sons, together with Junior Captain Masamichi and others, scattered rice around with great shouts, trying to see who could make the most noise, so much so indeed that the Bishop of the Jōdoji, present in his role as Protector, was forced to protect his own head and face with a fan for fear of being hit; this greatly amused the younger women.

The Doctor of Letters who read out the text from the classics was Chamberlain Hironari. Standing below the balustrade, he read out the opening passage from the *Records of the Historian*,[18] while behind him in two lines stood twenty men, ten of fifth and ten of sixth rank, twanging their bows.

What is known as the evening bath was really only a formal repetition of the first bath, and the ceremony was as before. I think there was a different reader: it may have been Munetoki, the Governor of Ise, reading the usual text from the *Classic of Filial Piety*. Takachika, I

17 Tigers are not indigenous to Japan, so this had probably arrived at court as a gift from either Korea or China, at least two hundred years before this event. It is probable that the head was held over the bath, its face reflected in the water to scare away evil influences, although there are some commentaries that suggest this is a skull actually dipped in the water. Whatever the case, it should be understood to be an extremely rare, talismanic object.

18 All the readings were from the Chinese classics. It is likely that a 'reading' in fact consisted of a formalized recitation in Sino-Japanese pronunciation, which would not have been readily understood without reference to the text itself, even without the twanging of the bows. The *Shih-chi* ('Records of the Historian') is the first Chinese Standard History, compiled by Ssu-ma Ch'ien and covering events in China from the beginnings to 100 BC.

heard, was the reader for the 'Emperor Wen' chapter from the *Records*, the three men taking turns over the seven-day period.[19]

The whole spectacle, with Her Majesty in spotless white setting off in contrast the vivid shapes and black hair of her ladies-in-waiting, seemed like a skilful black-and-white sketch that had come alive. I myself felt very ill at ease and self-conscious, so hardly ventured out during the day at all. Resting indoors, I observed the ladies as they passed from the rooms in the east wing over to the main building. Those who were allowed the forbidden colours[20] had mantles made from the same figured silk as their jackets, which gave them elegance but no individuality. Those to whom the colours were forbidden, especially the older ones among them, had been careful to avoid anything out of the ordinary and had dressed simply in beautiful robes of three or four layers, mantles of figured silk, and plain jackets; some had robes decorated with damask and gauze. Their fans were not gaudy in any way, and yet they had a certain elegance. They were inscribed with appropriate phrases, almost as if the women had all discussed the matter between themselves beforehand. Now, as they looked at each other, they suddenly realized how, although each one of them had tried to show some originality, those of a common age are bound to have common tastes. There was a strong atmosphere of rivalry. Their trains and jackets had, of course, been embroidered. The jackets had decorated cuffs; the silver thread stitched down the seams of the trains had been made to look like braid; and silver foil had been inlaid into the figured pattern on the fans. You felt as if you were gazing at mountains deep in snow in clear moonlight. It was so bright, indeed,

---

19 Murasaki again makes a point of telling us that she was not present. Her reference to the 'Emperor Wen' chapter here may be a mistake for the section on Emperor Wen in the *Chronicles of the Han*. We know this because other records of this event survive: see Appendix 2 for details.

20 The rules governing who could wear what colour were complicated and subject to constant change. According to the earliest specialized source we have, dated *c.* 1150, only women of a certain rank were allowed to wear yellow-green or red, but this restriction was limited to jackets of figured silk and printed trains. On this particular occasion, however, everyone is dressed in white, so the term may simply govern the type of material allowed.

that you could hardly distinguish anything, as if the room had been hung with mirrors.

On the evening of the third day,[21] the members of Her Majesty's staff, led by the Master of the Household, Tadanobu, took charge of the first celebration. Tadanobu presented Her Majesty with the food: a small aloes-wood table and silver bowls – I was not close enough to see more. Middle Counsellor Toshikata and Fujiwara no Sanenari presented clothing and bedding for the prince. Everything – the lining in the clothes chests, the wraps for the clothing itself, the chest covers and the stands – was of the same white material and the same design, and yet care had been taken to leave some individual trace. I presume that Takamasa, Governor of Ōmi, had taken care of all the other arrangements. The nobles were seated in the western gallery of the east wing, ranked in two rows from north to south; the senior courtiers sat in the southern gallery, ranked from west to east. Portable screens of white damask had been erected facing outwards along the blinds that divided the gallery from the central chamber.

The celebrations for the evening of the fifth day were arranged by His Excellency. It was the fifteenth of the month with a bright moon in a cloudless sky. Even the sight of the lowest menials, chattering to each other as they walked round lighting the fire baskets under the trees by the lake and arranging the food in the garden, seemed to add to the sense of occasion. Torchbearers stood everywhere at attention and the scene was as bright as day. Standing here and there in the shadow of the rocks or under the trees were those whom I took to be retainers of visiting nobles. They were wreathed in smiles and looked very pleased with themselves, as if they somehow felt that their own private prayers for the birth of this bright light into the world had come to fruition. Hardly surprising then that His Excellency's own retainers – even men

21 Celebrations were held on the third, fifth, seventh and ninth days after the birth, each time with a different group of courtiers in charge of the arrangements.

of minor importance among them such as those of fifth rank and below – were to be seen scurrying back and forth, bowing to everyone in sight and clearly very much aware of their own good fortune.

When the order was given for the food to be brought in, a procession of eight ladies dressed in white, their hair done up with white ribbon, carried in a series of white trays. The lady in charge of serving Her Majesty this evening was Miya no Naishi. She always had great presence, but with her hair combed up so that it fell over her shoulders she looked even more striking than usual; I remember in particular that part of her profile not hidden by her fan. The eight ladies who had their hair done up, Genshikibu, Kozaemon, Kohyōe, Tayū, Ōmuma, Komuma, Kohyōbu and Komoku – the most attractive young women – sat in two rows facing each other. It was certainly a sight to remember. It is in fact quite normal to have to put up one's hair when serving Her Majesty, but these women, who had been specially chosen by His Excellency for the occasion, could do nothing but complain about how dreadful it was to be so exposed; I thought they made themselves ridiculous.

The sight of thirty or more women sitting in rows in the double-span area to the east of the dais was most impressive. Servants carried in the ceremonial food. In front of the screens that now partitioned off the bath by the side door another set of screens had been set up facing south, and the food was arranged there on a pair of white cabinets.[22]

In the moonlight, which increased in intensity as the night wore on, sat servants, kitchen staff, hairdressers, maids and cleaners, some of whom I had never seen before. There were others, possibly the women in charge of the keys, who, despite somewhat inadequate dress and powder, fairly bristled with combs and looked terribly stiff and formal. They were all crowded on to the veranda, between the entrance to the back corridor and the bridge, making it impossible for anyone else to pass through.

When they had finished serving, the women went to sit down by the blinds. Everything was sparkling in the light of the flares but, even

22 See ground-plan 5 (Appendix 1) for a clearer picture of the layout at this point.

so, some women still stood out: Lady Ōshikibu wore a beautiful train and jacket, both embroidered with the Komatsubara scene at Mt Oshio.[23] She is the wife of the Governor of Michinokuni and His Excellency's envoy, you know. Lady Tayū had left her jacket as it was, but her train had a striking wave pattern printed on it in silver, not overly conspicuous but most pleasing to the eye. Ben no Naishi had a train printed with an unusual design, a crane standing in a silver sea-scape; as a symbol of longevity it was a perfect complement to the pine branches on the embroidery. Lady Shōshō's train was decorated with silver foil that was not quite up to the same standard as the others, and it became the subject of some adverse comment. By Lady Shōshō I mean the younger sister of Sukemitsu, the Governor of Shinano, a lady of long standing in His Excellency's employ.

Her Majesty looked so radiant this evening that it made one feel like showing her off, so I pushed open the screens which concealed the priest on night duty. 'I'm sure you will never be able to see the like again!' I remember saying. At this he left his devotions. 'Oh!' he murmured, rubbing his hands together and looking very pleased. 'You're too good, too good.'

The nobles left their seats and went on to the bridge where they began playing dice in the company of His Excellency. I hate it when they start betting. Poems were composed and we all prepared ourselves, reciting one just in case the cup should come round to the women:

> As we hand it round under a full moon,
> May this cup, shining with rare reflected light,
> Bring everlasting blessings.[24]

---

23 Komatsubara was an area just north-east of the capital often used for its poetic associations. This particular design may well have been based on the following congratulatory poem by the poet Ki no Tsurayuki: *Ah Ōhara, and Komatsubara at Oshio: may the trees soon grow tall and show us the face of immortality (Gosenshū*, commissioned 951, Poem 1374).

24 As the effect of this poem in Japanese relies on word-play (three examples in this case), it is difficult to reproduce in translation. Murasaki obviously thought it clever enough to record, despite the fact that she never had an opportunity to recite it.

We were whispering to each other how careful one had to be with not only the poem itself but also the recitation when in the presence of Major Counsellor Kintō,[25] but then in the end, perhaps because they were so busy and it was getting late, they retired before picking out any ladies.

Gifts were presented. The nobles were given robes for their women together with some of the prince's clothes and bedding, I think. Senior courtiers of fourth rank were each given a set of lined robes and trouser-skirts, those of fifth rank the robes only, and those of sixth rank just the trouser-skirts.

The next evening there was a beautiful moon and, as the weather was perfect, some of the younger women went out in a boat. Their black hair stood out in clear contrast against their white dresses – far more so than had they been wearing colours. Kodayū, Genshikibu, Miyagi no Jijū, Gosechi no Ben, Ukon, Kohyōe, Koemon, Muma, Yasurai, and the Lady from Ise had all been sitting near the veranda when Adviser of the Left Tsunefusa and His Excellency's second son Norimichi tried to entice them out on to the lake. Adviser of the Right Kanetaka was persuaded to pole them. Some of the women slipped away and stayed indoors, but they were probably a little jealous, for they kept on glancing outside from time to time. The shapes and faces reflecting the moonlight in the garden with its white sand were most intriguing.

We heard that a number of carriages had arrived at the northern guardhouse. It was the ladies from the Palace. I remember hearing that they included Tōzanmi, Lady Jijū, Lady Tōshōshō, Lady Muma, Lady Sakon, Lady Chikuzen, Lady Shō and Lady Ōmi, but I may have been mistaken since I did not know them all by sight. The women in the

---

25 This is Fujiwara no Kintō (966–1041), the arbiter of poetic taste at the time. It is interesting to note the importance placed on reciting poetry correctly. Sei Shōnagon has a similar passage, where she records her apprehension at having to reply to one of Kintō's poems. See I. Morris, *The Pillow Book of Sei Shōnagon* (London: Oxford University Press, 1967, vol. I, pp. 120–21; Penguin Classics, 1971, p. 135). Kintō's own (far more mundane) poem on this occasion can be found in the collection of his own poems (*Kintōshū*, Poem 23034): *Ah! See the peaceful face of the autumn moon; it brings the promise of a lengthy reign.*

boat came in looking flustered. His Excellency emerged to sit with the ladies. Very much at his ease, he bade them welcome and indulged in a little banter. Gifts were presented in accordance with rank.

The celebrations on the evening of the seventh day were held under the aegis of the court. Junior Captain Michimasa, acting as Imperial messenger, presented Her Majesty with a willow box which contained a scroll listing the gifts. She accepted it, passing it straight on to her attendants. Then the scholars from the Kangakuin[26] entered in procession and a list of those present was also given to Her Majesty. This too she passed on. Gifts must have also been given in return. The ceremony that evening was extremely elaborate and dreadfully noisy.

When I peeped in through the curtains that surrounded Her Majesty, far from giving the impression of grandeur one expected from someone fêted as 'Mother of the Land', she was reclining listlessly and looked pale and drawn, even more fragile, young and beautiful than ever, I thought. In the clear light of a small lamp hung inside the curtains her lovely complexion was of translucent delicacy; I realized that when her mass of hair was tied up it did indeed set off her face to advantage. But all this hardly needs comment, so I shall write of it no more.

The arrangements for this ceremony were the same as for the previous occasion. Gifts for the nobles, in the form of women's robes and the Prince's clothes, were handed out from behind the blinds. The senior courtiers, led by the two First Chamberlains, came up in order to receive them. The presents from the court included dresses, bed clothes and rolls of silk. Lady Tachibana, who had given the Prince his first breast, was presented with the usual dresses, and in addition a long robe of figured silk contained in a silver chest which was also covered,

26 The Kangakuin was a college founded by Fujiwara no Fuyutsugu in 821 for the purpose of educating members of the clan. As will be seen from Appendix 2, most other sources in fact record this procession as taking place on the third day rather than on the seventh. This would make more sense, because it would have been far more appropriate for scholars from this private clan institution to have participated in an event sponsored by Her Majesty's Household, as was the case on the third.

if I remember correctly, in white cloth. I heard she was also given another special gift besides, but I was not close enough to her to be able to see.

On the eighth day we all changed back into our coloured robes.

The celebrations on the evening of the ninth day were arranged by Yorimichi, now Master Elect of the Crown Prince's Household. Food was placed on a pair of white cabinets and arranged in a most unusual, up-to-date fashion. There was also a silver clothes-chest inlaid with a seascape design of large waves and Mt Hōrai, in itself nothing out of the ordinary and yet delicately fashioned so it caught the eye – but I fear if I single out everything for comment, I will never finish.

That night everything returned to normal. The dais was rehung with curtains that had the 'decayed wood' pattern printed on the facing. We all wore gowns of deep crimson. It was a change to see colours again, quite bewitching. The sheen on the gowns could be seen through the translucent gauze of the jackets and you could clearly distinguish people's figures.

That was the night Lady Koma had her embarrassing experience.[27]

Her Majesty was in convalescence until some time after the tenth of the tenth month. We waited on her night and day in rooms which lay to the west of the main hall.[28] His Excellency came to see the Prince at all hours, sometimes at midnight, sometimes at dawn. The wet nurse would be sound asleep; dead to the world, she would suddenly wake to find him rummaging around her breasts. I felt very sorry for her.

27 As we know from the account of this incident in the *Shōyūki* (see Appendix 2), it actually occurred on the seventeenth rather than the nineteenth. A serving lady called Koma no Takashina was the butt of much drunken revelry, Michinaga going so far as to take off one of his robes and offer it to her. At first she refused, but in the end she was forced to accept the gift. A visit to her apartments presumably followed.

28 The white dais had been removed on the eighteenth when everyone had changed back into colours, so only one dais remained. It was relocated to the western side of the eastern chamber. See ground-plan 6 (Appendix 1).

The child was really too small, but then it was only natural that His Excellency should want to lift the boy up in his arms and play with him to his heart's content. On one occasion the Prince went so far as to forget himself; His Excellency untied his cloak and hung it up to dry behind the dais.

'Look!' he chuckled. 'Peed all over me! Marvellous! And now to dry it – all our hopes come true!'

His Excellency was extremely persistent about the Prince Nakatsukasa business and kept pushing me, under the impression that I was in the Prince's favour.[29] I really had so many worries.

As the day for the imperial visit to the mansion approached, everything was repaired and polished. Rare chrysanthemums were ordered and transplanted. As I gazed out at them through the wraiths of morning mist – some fading to varying hues, others yellow and in their prime, all arranged in various ways – it seemed to me that old age might indeed be conquered. But then for some strange reason – if only my appetites were more mundane, I might find more joy in life, regain a little youth, and face it all with equanimity – seeing and hearing these marvellous, auspicious events only served to strengthen my yearnings. I felt downcast, vexed that nothing was turning out as I had hoped and that my misery simply seemed to increase.

'But why?' I asked myself. 'Now surely is the time to forget. It does me no good to fret, and besides, it will only make matters worse.'

As day dawned, I looked outside and saw the ducks playing about on the lake as if they had not a care in the world:

> Can I remain indifferent to those birds on the water?
> I too am floating in a sad uncertain world.

29 Prince Nakatsukasa, Tomohira (964–1009), seventh son of Emperor Murakami, was forty-five at the time and the 'business' concerned a possible marriage between his daughter and Michinaga's eldest son, Yorimichi. The marriage is discussed in some detail in Chapter 8 of the *Eiga monogatari* ('A Tale of Flowering Fortunes'), but there is surprisingly no mention of it in Michinaga's own diary. Why he should think that Murasaki had influence over the Prince is not known.

They too looked as though they were enjoying life but must suffer greatly, I thought.

I was in the midst of composing a reply to a note sent by Lady Koshōshō, when all of a sudden it became dark and started to rain. As the messenger was in a hurry, I finished it off with: 'and the sky too seems unsettled.' I must have included a rather lame verse, for that evening the messenger returned with a poem written on dark purple cloud-patterned paper:

> The skies at which I gaze and gaze are overcast;
> How is it that they too rain down tears of longing?

Unable to remember what I had written, I replied:

> It is the season for such rainy skies;
> Clouds may break, but these watching sleeves will never dry.

On the day of the imperial visit, His Excellency had the boats poled over to where he could inspect them. They had been specially made for the occasion. They were most impressive; you could almost imagine that the dragon and mythical bird on the prows were alive.[30] As we heard that the procession was to arrive at about eight in the morning, we had been fussing about with our dress and powder since early dawn. The nobles were to sit in the west wing so there was none of the usual commotion on our side of the mansion, but I was told that the women who served His Excellency's second daughter had been obliged to be more than usually careful about their dress.

Lady Koshōshō arrived at dawn, so we dressed and did our hair together. As we knew these affairs were inevitably delayed, we dawdled somewhat and were still waiting for some new fans to replace our own rather uninspiring ones when suddenly there came the sound of drums and we had to hurry over in a rather undignified manner.

30 Both these creatures had magic powers that prevented boats and ships from sinking in wind or waves. The fantastical shapes were copied from Chinese example. Here, of course, we are only talking of boats poled in the shallow garden lake. Once the ceremonies are under way, the musicians will play on the lake.

The water-music that greeted the Emperor was enchanting. As the procession approached, the bearers — despite being of low rank — hoisted the palanquin right up the steps and then had to kneel face down beneath it in considerable distress. 'Are we really that different?' I thought to myself as I watched. 'Even those of us who mix with nobility are bound by rank. How very difficult!'

A space to the west of the dais had been reserved for His Majesty and his chair was set up in the eastern part of the southern gallery. One span away, at the east end of the gallery, blinds had been hung north–south for the ladies-in-waiting to sit behind. Then the blind by the southernmost pillar was raised slightly to allow two handmaids to step forward. They were elegantly dressed with their hair up for the occasion, just as you might find in an exquisite Chinese painting.

Saemon no Naishi carried the sword. She was wearing a plain yellow-green jacket, a train shading at the hem, and a sash and waist-band with raised embroidery in orange and white checked silk. Her mantle had five cuffs of white lined with dark red, and her crimson gown was of beaten silk. Her form, her demeanour, and that part of her face that you could just see round her fan, gave her an impression of vitality and freshness.

Ben no Naishi carried the Imperial Jewel in a casket. Over a crimson gown she wore a mantle of light purple, and a train and jacket similar to Saemon no Naishi's. She was a petite, attractive woman and I was sorry to see her so embarrassed and nervous. She was by far the more stylish of the two, even down to her choice of fan. Her sash was of green and purple check. The sashes snaked and trailed around both women in dreamlike fashion; were those angels said to have descended from heaven to dance in ages past dressed like this? I asked myself.

The Imperial bodyguards, all impeccably dressed, were busy attending to the palanquin; they made a splendid sight. Chamberlain and Middle Captain Kanetaka it was who passed in the sword and jewel.

Looking around within the blinds, I could see those permitted the forbidden colours wearing the usual yellow-green and red jackets with trains of printed silk. Their mantles were mostly of dark red figured silk, except for Muma no Chūjō's which was light purple, I remember. Their gowns resembled a miscellany of autumn leaves of varying tints, and their lined robes were, as usual, of various colours: saffron of differing shades, purple lined with dark red, and yellow lined in green, some being of three rather than five layers.

Of those who were not permitted the colours, the older women wore plain jackets in yellow-green or dark red, each with five damask cuffs. Their robes were all of damask. The brightness of the wave pattern printed on their trains caught the eye, and their waistlines too were heavily embroidered. They had white robes lined with dark red in either three or five layers but of plain silk. The younger women wore jackets with five cuffs of various colours: white on the outside with dark red on yellow-green, white with just one green lining, and pale red shading to dark with one white layer interposed. They were all most intelligently arranged. I also noticed some specially decorated fans that looked very unusual.

At normal times of informality, you can usually identify someone who has been less than careful about her appearance, but on this occasion everyone had tried as hard as possible to dress well and to look as attractive as the next. Just as in a beautiful example of a Japanese scroll, you could hardly tell them apart. The only difference you could detect was between the older women and the younger ones, and then only because some had hair that was thinning a little, whereas others still had thick tresses. Yet, strangely enough, it seemed that one glance at that part of the face which showed above the fans was enough to tell whether or not a person were truly elegant. Those who still stood out among such women were indeed exceptional.

The five women from the Palace who had already been seconded to Her Majesty were in attendance: two handmaids, two palace ladies and one to serve the meal. When the order to proceed was given, Chikuzen and Sakyō, their hair done up in a bun, emerged from the same corner pillar as that used by the handmaids. They were not quite so angel-like. The latter wore a yellow-green jacket of plain silk with cuffs of white lined with pale green, and the former a jacket with five cuffs, white lined in dark red. They both wore the usual printed trains. The server was Lady Tachibana. I could not see her properly because she was hidden behind a pillar, but she too had her hair up and appeared to be wearing a yellow-green jacket and, in place of a mantle, yellow robes of Chinese damask lined with green.

His Excellency picked up the Prince and presented him to His Majesty. His Majesty in turn took him in his arms and as he did so the Prince gave a little whimper. Lady Saishō approached to present the sword. Then the Prince was taken across the central passage to Her Excellency's quarters in the western chamber. As His Majesty emerged, Lady Saishō returned to her seat.

'It was all so formal. I felt dreadfully nervous,' she said, and indeed she looked very flushed as she sat down. It made her look most attractive. Her clothes too showed evidence of a unique sensitivity to colour.

As the sun went down, the music and other entertainment was enchanting. The nobles sat in attendance upon His Majesty. Various dances were performed – the 'Dance of Ages', the 'Dance of Peace', and the 'Hall of Felicitation', the finale being the tune 'Great Joy'.[31] As the boats skirted the southern mound and receded into the distance, the sound of flutes and drums mingled with the wind in the pines deep in the trees to exquisite effect. The clear stream flowed pleasingly down to the lake, where the water rippled in the wind. It was a little cool by now and yet His Majesty wore only two underjackets. Lady Sakyō, obviously feeling chilly herself, expressed great concern for him; we all tried to hide our smiles.

'I remember,' said Lady Chikuzen, 'in the Dowager Empress's time there were so many imperial visits to the mansion. Ah such times!' and she broke into reminiscences. Fearing this was hardly a propitious way to behave in the circumstances, the others avoided responding, almost as if there were an invisible curtain hung between her and us. She certainly did look as though, given the slightest encouragement, she would have burst into tears.

31 These were some of the many *bugaku* court dances performed on such occasions. The provenance of each dance was generally known and in this case all are of Chinese origin. In view of the fact that Michinaga's diary records 'Chinese and Korean, two dances each', Murasaki may be mistaken here.

Just as the music for His Majesty reached a particularly interesting passage, the Prince gave a sweet little cry. 'Listen!' exclaimed Akimitsu, Minister of the Right, in admiration. 'The Dance of Ages harmonizes with his cries!' Major Counsellor Kintō, with some others present, recited 'For ten thousand ages and a thousand autumns'.[32]

'Ah!' said His Excellency, bursting into maudlin tears. 'How could we ever have considered previous visits so marvellous? This surpasses them all!' An obvious enough remark, perhaps, but most gratifying that he recognized his own good fortune.

His Excellency went over to the west wing. His Majesty entered and asked the Minister of the Right to appear before him and write out the list of promotions. All those of Her Majesty's and His Excellency's officers who were eligible were promoted. The preliminary list had, I understand, been prepared in advance by First Chamberlain Michikata.

To give thanks for the birth of a new prince, the nobles of the main Fujiwara clan all bowed in obeisance before His Majesty. Those who were from a different branch of the Fujiwara, however, were excluded. Then Tadanobu, as Commander of the Gate Guards of the Right – the Master of Her Majesty's Household, you know – who had just been made Superintendent of the new prince's office, led the others in a formal dance of thanksgiving, together with Sanenari, who, as Assistant Master of the Prince's Household, had also been promoted that day.

The Emperor went in to see Her Majesty, but it was not long before there were shouts that it was getting late and that the palanquin was ready to leave. He returned to the Palace.

The next morning, even before the mist had cleared, a messenger came from the Palace. I slept in late and so missed seeing him. Today the Prince was to have his head shaved for the first time; it had apparently been postponed on purpose until after the imperial visit.

32 This phrase is part of a poem that can be found in the 'Celebration' section of the *Wakan rōeishū*, an anthology of well-known Chinese and Japanese verses compiled by the very person who is reciting it here – Fujiwara no Kintō, whom we have previously met (see note 25). The poem reads: *No limit to the delight at a time of celebration; For ten thousand ages and a thousand autumns the pleasure never ends.*

Today was also the day when they decided who were to be appointed as steward, superintendent and ladies-in-waiting to the Prince. I was most vexed because I had been given no prior warning.[33]

For these last few days the furnishings in Her Majesty's rooms had been unusually sparse, but now everything was changed and looked splendid once again. Now that the long-awaited birth had turned out well,[34] Her Excellency would come in as soon as dawn had broken and take care of the baby in a manner I found most affecting.

That evening there was a bright moon. The Assistant Master of the Prince's Household, Sanenari, who was perhaps intending to ask a lady-in-waiting to express his own special thanks to Her Majesty, finding that the area by the side door was wet with water from the bath with no sign of anyone being around, came over instead to Miya no Naishi's room at the eastern end of our corridor.[35]

'Is anyone there?' he inquired.

He then moved to the middle room and pushed up the top half of the shutters that I had left unlocked.

'Anyone here?' he asked again. At first I gave no reply, but then he was joined by Tadanobu and, thinking it seemed a little churlish of me to continue ignoring them, I gave a sign of having heard. Neither of them seemed the least put out.

'You ignore me but pay great attention to the Master of the Household,' said Sanenari with a touch of sarcasm. 'Understandable, I suppose, but nevertheless to be deplored. Why the emphasis on rank here?' And with that he started singing 'the hallowed nature of today' in a rather attractive voice.[36]

33 Why? Murasaki must have been hoping for some advancement for one of her close relatives, perhaps her ill-starred brother, and she had lost the opportunity to exert any influence she might have had.

34 From her parents' point of view, the birth certainly was 'long-awaited'. Shōshi had entered the Palace in 999, at which point she had been eleven, but Emperor Ichijō (980–1011) already nineteen: she was now twenty-one.

35 This particular room has been Murasaki's up to this point and it is not clear why she has moved. As the following passage makes clear, however, she must have moved into the middle room at some stage. See ground-plan 2 (Appendix 1).

36 This line is from a *saibara* or folk song. These were adopted at court and given a formal accompaniment in the Chinese manner. All the other songs mentioned in the diary from this point on are also *saibara*.

28

As it was now the dead of night, the moon seemed very bright.

'Do take away the bottom of the lattice!' they insisted. Despite the fact we were in private, I refused. I felt it would be embarrassing to have these nobles demean themselves in such a manner, and while frivolous behaviour by someone younger might be overlooked and put down to inexperience, I could hardly be so reckless, I told myself.

The fiftieth-day celebrations took place on the first of the eleventh month. Her Majesty was surrounded by her women, who all came to the Palace attired, as usual, for the occasion. I remember thinking how much it resembled an illustration of a formal competition. She was sitting to the east of the dais, which was divided off by a line of overlapping curtains that ran from the sliding screen at the back to the gallery pillar at the front, with the ceremonial meal placed in front of her, I think.[37] Her own food was laid somewhat to the west on the usual aloes-wood tray and a kind of stand; I could not see exactly. The server was Lady Saishō. The women who brought in the food had their hair dressed with pins and ribbons. The Prince, whose food was placed to the east, was served by Lady Dainagon. His tiny platter, bowls, chopstick holders, and the decorated centrepiece looked like toys made for a doll. The blinds by the eastern gallery were raised a little to allow those whose duty it was – Ben no Naishi, Lady Naka-tsukasa, and Lady Kochūjō – to bring in the food. I did not have a very good view because I was sitting at the back.

That evening wet nurse Shō was awarded the forbidden colours. She was very composed as she carried the Prince over to the curtained dais. Her Excellency then took the child from her, and as she moved out into the centre of the room, she looked quite magnificent in the light of the torches. I was full of admiration at how carefully she had dressed in a red jacket and a plain printed train. Her Majesty wore a mantle of light purple with five cuffs under a somewhat less

---

37 For a clearer picture of what is going on at this point see ground-plan 7 (Appendix 1). The records translated in Appendix 2 are particularly detailed for this ceremony.

formal robe of dark red. His Excellency offered the rice cakes to the Prince.[38]

The nobles were seated as usual in the western gallery of the east wing. The other two Ministers, Akimitsu and Kinsue, were also present. Then some of them moved on to the bridge and started carousing again. Various boxes and containers were brought over by attendants from His Excellency's quarters and lined up along the balustrade. The light from the firebrands in the garden was not sufficient, so Junior Captain Masamichi and others were ordered to stand there with torches so that everyone could clearly see. The gifts were due to be transported to the Table Room in the Palace, so they had to be rushed over this evening because the Palace was due to enter a period of abstinence from tomorrow.

The Master of Her Majesty's Household came up to the blinds.

'The nobles at your service!' he announced.

'Understood,' came the reply. So the nobles entered, led by His Excellency. They sat in order of rank from just east of the main steps right round to the front of the side door. Then the ladies-in-waiting, who were sitting in rows of two or three facing them, went to their respective blinds and rolled them up. Sat in order were Lady Dainagon, Lady Saishō, Lady Koshōshō and Miya no Naishi. The Minister of the Right, Akimitsu, moved in closer and pulled the curtains apart at the seams, nearly ripping them.[39]

'He's far too old for such goings on!' we whispered among ourselves, but he took not the slightest notice. Instead, he picked up a fan and made a number of smutty remarks. The Master of the Household took some rice wine over to where they were sitting. They sang 'Minoyama', and the music, though impromptu, was most attractive.

Major Captain Sanesuke was leaning against a pillar two spans to

38 It was the custom for the father or grandfather to offer little rice cakes to the child on such occasions, merely a ceremonial gesture.
39 The men are sitting on the veranda facing inwards, while the women are sitting in the southern gallery facing outwards: see ground-plan 7 (Appendix 1). The blinds have been rolled up but the women are still hidden by curtains which were joined by seams loose enough to allow things to be passed through, or to act as peepholes. It is these that Akimitsu is now pulling apart to get a better view.

the east, checking the hems and sleeves of our robes. He was quite unlike the others.[40] Under the impression that he was befuddled with drink, we made light of him, and some of the women, certain they would never be recognized, started flirting with him a little, only to discover that far from being flamboyant, he seemed to be a paragon of propriety. He was waiting with some consternation for his turn to come round, but made do in the end with the usual congratulatory phrases.

Major Counsellor Kintō poked his head in.

'Excuse me,' he said. 'Would our little Murasaki be in attendance by any chance?'

'I cannot see the likes of Genji here, so how could she be present?' I replied.[41]

'Assistant Master Third Rank!' called out His Excellency. 'Take the cup!' Sanenari stood up and, seeing that his father, the Minister of the Centre, was present, made sure that he came up via the steps from the garden.[42] Seeing this, his father burst into tears. Middle Counsellor Elect Takaie, who was leaning against a corner pillar, started pulling at Lady Hyōbu's robes and singing dreadful songs. His Excellency said nothing.

Realizing that it was bound to a terribly drunken affair this evening, Lady Saishō and I decided to retire once the formal part was over. We were just about to leave when His Excellency's two sons, together

40 This gentleman is Fujiwara no Sanesuke, author of the *Shōyūki*, a court diary written in Sino-Japanese that covers the years 982-1032, part of which is translated in Appendix 2. Sanesuke was a well-known critic of Michinaga's opulence and he may be looking at the women's robes with a jaundiced eye, marking up yet another instance of extravagance.

41 This is the only reference in the diary to the name Murasaki. It is, of course, a nickname associated with the fictional heroine of the *Tale of Genji* and this little vignette probably records its genesis: it would not be surprising if a name first bestowed by the eminent Kintō were quickly to gain currency.

42 The situation here is a little vague. The nobles are sitting on the veranda, which is quite narrow, so there would be no space to walk behind them. When asked to take the cup, Assistant Master Fujiwara no Sanenari carefully avoids walking in front of his father, goes instead down the steps at the east end of the veranda, walks along the garden and comes up the centre steps. His father, who is drunk, bursts into tears on seeing how his son can observe the correct formalities in such a situation.

with Kanetaka and some other gentlemen, came into the eastern gallery and started to create a commotion. We hid behind the dais, but His Excellency pulled back the curtains and we were both caught.

'A poem each for the Prince!' he cried. 'Then I'll let you go!'

Being in such a quandary, I recited:

> How on this fiftieth day can we possibly count
> The countless years of our prince's reign!

'Oh! Splendid!' he said, reciting it twice to himself; then he gave a very quick reply:

> Had I as many years as the crane, then might I count
> How many thousand years his eternal reign would be.

Even in his inebriated state, his mind was still on the future of the Prince. I was both moved and reassured. If His Excellency looked on the boy with such favour, then he must indeed be ensured a brilliant reign. Even I, in my own insignificant way, was filled with the thought of his future fortunes, for which a thousand years would be too brief.

'Did Her Majesty hear that?' he said proudly. 'One of my better ones! I think I make a very good papa for an empress. And she's not bad for the daughter of a man like me either! Mother must think herself very fortunate knowing what a brilliant husband she has!' Such behaviour, it would seem, could be put down to excessive drinking. But he was far from being incapable and, although I myself felt a little apprehensive, Her Majesty listened to him in good humour. Her Excellency, however, perhaps unable to endure it any longer, made as if to leave.

'Mother will scold me if I fail to see her off, you know!' he said, rushing straight out through the curtained dias. 'Terribly rude of me, my dear, but then you owe it all to your father in any case, don't you!' he mumbled, at which everyone laughed.

The time for the return to the Palace was approaching, but we were constantly rushed off our feet. Her Majesty was involved in her book-binding, and so first thing every morning we had to go to her quarters to choose paper of various colours and to write letters of request to people, enclosing copies of the stories. We were also kept busy night and day sorting and binding work that had already been finished.

'What on earth are you doing in such cold weather?' asked His Excellency. 'You're meant to be resting!' Nevertheless, from time to time he would bring her good thin paper, brushes and ink. He even brought an inkstone. When the others found out that Her Majesty had given it to me, they all complained loudly. I had obtained it by going behind their backs, they said. Despite this, she made me another present of excellent coloured paper and some brushes.

Then, while I was in attendance, His Excellency sneaked into my room and found a copy of the Tale that I had asked someone to bring from home for safekeeping. It seems that he gave the whole thing to his second daughter. I no longer had the fair copy in my possession and was sure that the version she now had with her would hurt my reputation.[43]

The baby was beginning to make a few sounds, so it was only natural that His Majesty was getting somewhat impatient.

Seeing the water birds on the lake increase in number day by day, I thought to myself how nice it would be if it snowed before we got back to the Palace – the garden would look so beautiful; and then, two days later, while I was away on a short visit, lo and behold, it did snow. As I watched the rather drab scene at home, I felt both depressed and confused. For some years now I had existed from day to day in listless fashion, taking note of the flowers, the birds in song, the way the skies change from season to season, the moon, the frost and snow, doing

---

43 The stories mentioned earlier that Her Majesty was having copied may or may not have been by Murasaki, but there can be little doubt that this particular reference is to the *Tale of Genji*. The fact that copies would have taken months of hard work to produce, that they could so easily go astray like this, and that many of them may simply have been drafts rather than the finished product makes it all the more incredible that her work, in particular, has survived.

little more than registering the passage of time. How would it all turn out? The thought of my continuing loneliness was unbearable, and yet I had managed to exchange sympathetic letters with those of like mind – some contacted via fairly tenuous connections – who would discuss my trifling tales and other matters with me; but I was merely amusing myself with fictions, finding solace for my idleness in foolish words. Aware of my own insignificance, I had at least managed for the time being to avoid anything that might have been considered shameful or unbecoming; yet here I was, tasting the bitterness of life to the very full.

I tried reading the Tale again, but it did not seem to be the same as before and I was disappointed. Those with whom I had discussed things of mutual interest – how vain and frivolous they must consider me now, I thought; and then, ashamed that I could even contemplate such a remark, I found it difficult to write to them. Those in whose eyes I had wished to be of some consequence undoubtedly thought of me now as no more than a common lady-in-waiting who would treat their letters with scant respect; that they were unable to fathom my true feelings was only to be expected, but nevertheless it rankled, and, although I did not break with them entirely, there were many with whom I ceased to correspond as a matter of course. There were others who no longer came to see me, assuming that I was now of no fixed abode. Indeed everything, however slight, conspired to make me feel as if I had entered a different world. Being at home only served to make matters worse, and I was most forlorn.

It struck me as a sad truth that the only people left to me were those of my constant companions at court for whom I felt a certain affection, and those with whom I could exchange a secret or two, with whom I happened to be on good terms at the present moment. In particular I missed Lady Dainagon, who would often talk to me as we lay close by Her Majesty in the evenings. Had I then indeed succumbed to life at court?

I sent her the following:

How I long for those waters on which we lay,
A longing keener than the frost on a duck's wing.

To which she replied:

> Awakening to find no friend to brush away the frost,
> The mandarin duck longs for her mate at night.[44]

When I saw how elegantly it was written, I realized what an accomplished woman she was.

Others wrote, telling me how Her Majesty was so sorry that I could not be with her to see the snow. I also received a note from Her Excellency.

'You obviously did not mean it when you said you would only be away for a short while,' she wrote. 'I presume you are prolonging it on purpose since I tried to stop you.' She may not have been serious, but I had promised and she had given me leave to go, so I felt obliged to return.


Her Majesty returned to the Palace on the seventeenth. We had been told to be ready at eight in the evening, but the night wore on. Some thirty of us, dressed in formal attire with our hair done up but indistinguishable from each other in the darkness, took our places in the southern gallery. We were separated by the side door from the ten or more women from the Palace; they were seated in the eastern gallery to the east of the main chamber.

Her Majesty shared a palanquin with Miya no Senji. Behind them in a decorated carriage came Her Excellency and wet nurse Shō carrying the baby prince. Lady Dainagon and Lady Saishō came next in a carriage with gold fittings, and they in turn were followed by Lady Koshōshō and Miya no Naishi. I rode behind them with Muma no Chūjō, but she seemed resentful of my presence. Why should she be so high and mighty, I remember asking myself, vexed at the pettiness of court life. We were followed by Lady Jijū from the Office of Grounds and Ben no Naishi, and they in turn were followed by

---

**44** Mandarin ducks were supposed always to go around in inseparable pairs. This common metaphor for lovers originally came from Chinese literature but had by this time become firmly part of the Japanese poetic vocabulary. These poems should be seen as forming a conventional exchange between close friends – nothing more.

Saemon no Naishi and Lady Shikibu – His Excellency's envoy. After that there was no fixed order and everyone rode with whom she pleased.

When we finally arrived, the moon was so bright that I was embarrassed to be seen and knew not where to hide. I allowed Muma no Chūjō to go on ahead of me, but when I saw how she was stumbling along, not knowing where she was going, I realized what a sorry sight I must be presenting to those behind me.

As I lay down to rest in my room, which was third from the end in one of the outer galleries,[45] Lady Koshōshō came in to commiserate with me on how tiresome the whole affair had been. We discarded our outer robes, which had gone stiff with the cold, and put on some thick padded clothes instead. I was adding some charcoal to the burner and complaining how miserable it was to feel so chilled to the marrow, when who should drop by to pay their respects but Adviser Sanenari, Tsunefusa, Adviser of the Left, and Middle Captain Kinnobu, one after the other. They were rather unwelcome. I had hoped to have been left in peace that evening, but word must have got around.

'We'll come again early tomorrow morning. It's bitterly cold tonight; we're frozen!' they said somewhat offhandedly, leaving by the back entrance on our side. As they hurried away on their respective paths, I wondered what kind of women were waiting for them at home. Not that I was thinking so much of myself as of Lady Koshōshō: she was elegant and attractive by any standards, and yet here she was brooding over the melancholies of life. Fate seems to have treated her most unfairly ever since her father retired.[46]

*

45 The palace to which Her Majesty returns is not the main Imperial Palace but the much smaller mansion at Ichijō nearby. The Imperial Palace itself had been burned to the ground on Kankō 2 (1005).11.15 and, although rebuilding started a year later, it was not actually reoccupied until Kankō 8 (1011).8.11. For details of the Ichijō Palace see ground-plan 8 (Appendix 1).
46 Lady Koshōshō's father had retired from active life as early as 987 and she had been brought up by her mother. This lack of a male relative with the proper court connections would have been seen as a major impediment to making a good marriage.

The next morning Her Majesty held a close inspection of the gifts she had received the night before. The accessories in the comb boxes were so indescribably beautiful I could have gazed at them for ever. There was, in addition, another pair of boxes. In the top tray of one of them were some booklets made of white patterned paper: the *Kokinshū*, *Gosenshū* and *Shūishū*, each in five volumes, four sections to a volume,[47] copied by Middle Counsellor Yukinari and the priest Enkan. The covers were of fine silk and the ties were of similar imported material. In the bottom tray lay a number of personal poetry collections by poets old and new; poets such as Yoshinobu and Motosuke.[48] Those in the hands of Enkan and the Middle Counsellor were, of course, for safe keeping, but these other collections were for more everyday use; I do not know who had copied them, but they were of unusually modern design.

The Gosechi dancers arrived on the twentieth.[49] Her Majesty presented Adviser Sanenari with dresses for his dancer. She also gave Kanetaka, Adviser of the Right, the cord pendants that he had requested. We took the opportunity to give them both some incense in a set of boxes with artificial plum branches attached as decoration, to spur on their rivalry. I knew full well how hard the young dancers had prepared this year in comparison to normal years when things were

47 These books are the first three imperial anthologies of Japanese poetry: the *Kokinshū* was compiled *c.* 905, the *Gosenshū c.* 951, and the *Shūishū c.* 1005.

48 Ōnakatomi no Yoshinobu (921?–991) and Kiyohara no Motosuke (908–990) both took part in the compilation of the *Gosenshū*. It is not clear here whether Murasaki thought of these men as 'old' or 'new'.

49 The Gosechi dances were always performed over a period of four days late in the eleventh month. This year there were, as usual, four dancers, the daughters of Fujiwara no Sanenari, Fujiwara no Kanetaka, Takashina no Naritō and Fujiwara no Nakakiyo. The ceremonies began on the second day of the Ox (in this case the twentieth) when the four dancers would formally enter the Palace, each with a retinue of some ten attendants. It is this formal entrance that is being described here. In the evening they would perform the Dais Rehearsals. On the following day a banquet was held for the Imperial Rehearsals. The third day saw a presentation by the young girls (about ten years old) who were in attendance on the dancers, and the Festivals of the First Fruits were held that evening. The main Gosechi dances were performed on the fourth day.

usually done in such a hurry, so as they entered the glare of the torches that lined the standing screen opposite Her Majesty's rooms on the east side – they were more exposed than they would have been in broad daylight – all I could think of was what a dreadful ordeal it must be for them. The same misfortune had been visited on us as well, of course, but at least we had been spared the torches and the direct stares of the senior courtiers, for we had been surrounded by curtains to ward off the curious. In general, however, we must have presented a similar spectacle. I shudder to recall it.

The ladies in attendance on Naritō's dancer wore brocade jackets that stood out brilliantly even in the darkness of the night. They wore so many layers they seemed to have difficulty in moving, so the senior courtiers did what they could to help them. His Majesty came over to watch from our side of the building and His Excellency stole over as well and stood to the north of the sliding door;[50] this was rather inconvenient, since it meant we could not do exactly as we wished.

The attendants for Nakakiyo's dancer were all chosen to be exactly the same height and were pronounced to be every bit as magnificent and splendid as their rivals. Those in the Adviser of the Right's party had arranged everything perfectly; they even included two cleaning maids whose very stiffness made them seem a little provincial, bringing a smile to everyone's lips.

Last in line was the party belonging to Adviser Sanenari. Perhaps I was imagining things, but they all appeared particularly well dressed. There were ten attendants. The hems of their robes cascaded out from beneath the blinds which had been lowered in the outer gallery. The effect was not ostentatious: on the contrary, they looked extremely attractive in the glow of the lights.

On the morning of the twenty-first the senior courtiers came to pay their respects. It was the same every year of course, but perhaps because they had been away from the Palace for some months now,

50 It is not clear where this door is. If one assumes that Murasaki and the other ladies-in-waiting are sitting in the southern wing looking south, Michinaga must be standing just to their right. See ground-plan 8 (Appendix 1).

the younger women were all agog; and this despite the fact that ceremonial cloaks were not worn that day.[51]

That evening Naritō, as Assistant Master of the Crown Prince's Household, was summoned and presented with incense piled high in a large box. Nakakiyo, as Governor of Owari, was given a similar gift by Her Excellency. Her Majesty went over that evening to see the Imperial Rehearsals, I think it was. Because the baby prince was with her, there was much casting of rice and shouting of spells; quite different from usual.

I felt depressed and went to my room for a while to rest. I had intended to go over later if I felt better, but then Kohyōe and Kohyōbu came in and sat themselves down by the hibachi. 'It's so crowded over there, you can hardly see a thing!' they complained. His Excellency appeared.

'What do you think you're all doing, sitting around like this?' he said. 'Come along with me!'

I did not really feel up to it but went at his insistence.

I was watching the dancers, thinking how tense they looked, when suddenly the Governor of Owari's daughter took ill and had to retire; it was like watching a dream unfold. When it was all over, Her Majesty returned to her apartments.

The younger nobles could now talk of nothing but the attractiveness of the young dancers' apartments.

'Did you notice how the decoration on the edges and tops of each blind is a different design for each room? And the way they do their hair, the way they move around – they are all quite different from each other!'

The way they go on like this does annoy me.


Even in normal years the young girl attendants feel self-conscious when presenting themselves in front of His Majesty, so how much

51 Murasaki is here referring to the white cloaks dyed with indigo patterns that were connected with Shintō ritual and that were worn for the Gosechi ceremonies but only for the last two days of the event.

worse it must have been for them this year, I thought; I was both apprehensive and eager to see them.[52] As they finally stepped forward together I was, for some reason, overcome with emotion and felt dreadfully sorry for them. Not that I was closely tied to any one of them in particular, mind you. Was it because their patrons were so convinced that their girls were the best that, look as I would, I found it difficult to distinguish between them? Someone more in the know about fashion would have been able to detect differences at once, of course. And with all those young nobles around and the girls not allowed so much as a fan to hide behind in broad daylight, I felt somehow concerned for them, convinced that, although they may have been able to deal with the situation both in terms of rank and intelligence, they must surely have found the pressures of constant rivalry daunting; silly of me, perhaps.

Naritō's little girl looked very attractive in her pale-green coat, but the way Adviser Sanenari had dressed his girl in a red coat was enviable: it made a perfect contrast with her maid's yellow-green jacket. Of the two, the former seemed the plainer.

Adviser Kanetaka's girl stood very straight and had beautiful hair, but she was rather too forward, which caused some adverse comment. All four of them were wearing deep red underjackets and mantles of various colours. Three of them had coats with five cuffs, but the Governor of Owari's girl had a coat dyed light purple throughout, which made her look most elegant and attractive by contrast; its sheen and the way it blended in with the other dresses was most impressive.

As the Chamberlain of Sixth Rank and some other men came forward to take their fans, one of the maids, a very attractive girl, took it into her head to throw hers towards them. It was not an immodest gesture but not very ladylike either. But then, if I were ever asked to present myself like that in front of everyone, no doubt I too would prove equally as gauche; I, who never imagined I would be as much in

---

52 We are now in the third day of the ceremonies and Murasaki is describing the Imperial Viewing of the Girl Attendants. The dancers themselves rested on this day, but one young girl, with an older woman in attendance, was chosen from each party to perform before the Emperor. In contrast to the two previous occasions, this presentation took place in the daytime.

the public eye as I am even now. And yet feelings can be so fickle – they shift before your very eyes. 'From now on,' I told myself, 'I know my shamelessness shall be such that I will become quite used to life at court, inured to showing myself openly to others.' My future rose up before me like a dream and I began to think unwonted thoughts; I became quite upset and found the ceremonies much less interesting than usual.

The rooms occupied by Adviser Sanenari's party were right across from Her Majesty's apartments. Looking over the top of the screen, you could see the edging on the blinds that had caused so much comment. We could also hear snatches of conversation.

'Lady Sakyō seems to be very much at home with the ladies of the First Consort,'[53] said Adviser Kanetaka, revealing that he knew her of old. Junior Captain Masamichi also remembered her. 'That was Lady Sakyō the other night sitting on the east side among the attendants,' he said. Somehow all this came to the ears of Her Majesty's ladies, who thought it most interesting.

'Well, we can hardly just ignore it,' they said. 'Fancy someone who used to lord it in the Palace returning in such a manner! She must be trying to remain incognito. We must disillusion her!' and with that in mind they chose from the many fans in Her Majesty's collection one with a coloured painting of Mt Hōrai; they did it deliberately, but did she realize what it was meant to signify?[54] They placed the open fan on the lid of a box, arranged a dancer's cord pendants around it, and added a curved comb tied across the ends with a strip of ceremonial white paper.[55]

53 The First Consort was Fujiwara no Gishi (Yoshiko), Kinsue's daughter, also known as Kokiden. Apparently Lady Sakyō used to be in her service, left for some reason, and has now returned as an attendant for Sanenari's daughter. Sanenari was Gishi's younger brother.
54 Mt Hōrai was a symbol of longevity, used here no doubt as a specific reminder to Lady Sakyō that she was not getting any younger.
55 The ceremonial white paper was attached to the headdress worn by the Gosechi dancers, and at the Imperial Viewing of the Girl Attendants the selection of a comb was a mark of special favour. Apparently, the younger the woman, the greater the curvature on the comb.

'She's not as young as she used to be, you know!' said one of the younger nobles, bending it even more so that the ends nearly met in a dreadfully up-to-date fashion. They also prepared a roll of *kurobō* scent, cut both ends untidily, and then wrapped it in two sheets of white paper making it into a sort of folded letter. Lady Tayū was asked to write the following:

> Among the many ladies at the 'Banquet of the Flushed Faces'
> Your pendants were a source of shining admiration.[56]

'If you are going to give her a present like that,' said Her Majesty, 'you ought to make it more attractive; add some more fans or something.' 'No,' the women replied. 'It would not do to make it too exaggerated. If it were a gift from Your Majesty, there would be none of these hidden allusions in any case. This is our own little private affair.'

They sent as a messenger a woman who would not be recognized. 'A letter from Lady Chūnagon! From the First Consort's apartments, for Lady Sakyō!' she said in a loud voice as she passed it through the blinds. We were all worried lest she be caught, but she came hurrying back. Apparently someone had asked her where she had come from but no one had doubted her reply when she had said she had come from the First Consort's quarters.

Nothing of any real interest had happened during these last few days, but even so, once the festivities were over, the Palace suddenly felt dreary; things were only enlivened by some rehearsals on the night of the twenty-fourth.[57] I can just imagine how bored the younger nobles must have felt after all the excitement.

---

56 The Banquet of the Flushed Faces took place on the fourth and last day of the festivities. Somewhere in the course of the previous passage Murasaki has moved on to describe events on the twenty-third.

57 These were the penultimate *gagaku* rehearsals for the Special Festival at the Kamo Shrines, which was held on the last day of the Cock in the eleventh month (which fell this year on the twenty-eighth).

Even the Takamatsu sons were allowed into the women's apartments after Her Majesty's return to the Palace.[58] It was extremely annoying to have them traipsing in and out all the time, although, on the pretext of being too old for it all, I made myself scarce. Obviously the Gosechi ceremonies had made very little impression on them; instead they hung around the skirts of Yasurai, Kohyōe and the others, twittering away and making a general nuisance of themselves.

The imperial messenger for the Special Festival at the Kamo Shrines was His Excellency's fifth son, Middle Captain Elect Norimichi. It was a day of abstinence at the Palace and so His Excellency came the evening before and stayed overnight. The nobles and the young men who were to perform the dances also stayed at the Palace, with the result that the area around the women's quarters was pandemonium all night.

Early the next morning retainers from Kinsue, Minister of the Centre, arrived to hand over a gift to His Excellency's men: it was a silver book box lying on the lid that we had sent the previous day.[59] Packed inside was a mirror, an aloes-wood comb and a silver comb, all apparently for the imperial messenger to dress his hair. Embossed on the top of the box in reed-like script[60] was what appeared to be a reply to our 'cord pendants' poem, but two letters had been left out and it looked a little odd. Matters seem to have taken a strange turn. I remember hearing later that the Minister had made this formal gift in the belief that the first present had come from Her Majesty. It had only been a trifling joke on our part and I was sorry to see that it had been taken so seriously.

Her Excellency also came to the Palace to watch the imperial

58 The children of Michinaga's second wife Meishi, called Takamatsu after a mansion that had belonged to her father, Minamoto no Takaakira. They had kept their distance until now because the Tsuchimikado mansion belonged to Michinaga's first wife, Rinshi. Once Shōshi's retinue returned to the palace at Ichijō, they were again allowed free rein. As they were young men rather than boys, Yorimune (16), Akinobu (15) and Yoshinobu (14), it is not surprising that Murasaki was somewhat put out.

59 The lid is the one that they had sent to Lady Sakyō. Kinsue, who takes it upon himself to make a return gift, was Gishi's father.

60 A form of rebus writing whereby a poem was hidden in a sketch of reeds, rocks and water.

messenger depart. Seeing him there looking very grown-up and imposing with artificial wisteria flowers in his hair, his old wet-nurse Lady
Kura had no eyes for the dancers; she just gazed at him, tears running
down her cheeks.

Because of the abstinence at the Palace, they all returned from the
shrine at about two the following morning, so the dances performed
on their return were kept to a mere formality. Kanetoki had been
superb in the role of dancer in past years, but this year he seemed very
uncertain in his movements.[61] Despite the fact that I hardly knew him,
I felt sorry for him and it gave me much on which to reflect.

I returned to the Palace on the twenty-ninth of the twelfth month.[62]
Now I come to think of it, it was on this very night that I first entered
service at court. When I remember what a daze I was in then I find
my present somewhat blasé attitude quite uncomfortable.

It was very late. Her Majesty was in seclusion, so I did not go to see
her but lay down to rest on my own. I could hear the women talking
in the next room. 'How different it is here in the Palace! At home
everyone would be asleep but here it's the constant footsteps that keep
one awake!' they said immodestly.

>  As does the year, so do my days draw to an end;
>  How desolate the sounds of the wind in my heart

I murmured to myself.

On the last night of the year the ceremony of casting out devils[63] was
over very early, so I was resting in my room, blackening my teeth and

61 Owari no Kanetoki was a famous dancer of *kagura*, religious dances. This may well
have been his last Kamo Shrine dance, because Michinaga's diary records that he was
too ill to dance it the following year, 1009.

62 There is a gap of about one month at this point. A number of important ceremonies
were held during this period, but either Murasaki seems not to have found them worth
recording, or the record has been lost. Perhaps she returned home soon after the Gosechi dances in the eleventh month and spent the whole month away from the Palace.

63 This rite, known as *tsuina*, involved the casting of rice, beans and spells to usher out
evil spirits. It was the last of the year's ceremonies.

putting on a light powder, when Ben no Naishi came in, chatted for a while and then fell asleep.

Takumi, the maid, was sitting just outside in the corridor, intent on teaching Ateki how to pinch the hems of a dress she had just made, when suddenly there was uproar from the direction of Her Majesty's quarters. I shook Ben no Naishi but she took time to wake up. The crying and wailing was terrible to hear, and I was beside myself. I thought at first it was a fire, but no, it was something else.

'Come on!' I said, urging Takumi to take the lead. 'Whatever it is, Her Majesty is in her room tonight. We must go and see if she is all right.' Finally I managed to shake Ben no Naishi out of her slumbers and the three of us went over, trembling in fear and apprehension. What should we find but two women sitting there with no clothes on, Yugei and Kohyōbu! When I realized what had happened, I felt even more upset.

The menials had all retired and both Her Majesty's servants and the guards had left as soon as the ceremony was over. We clapped our hands and shouted, but to no avail. A serving girl was called out from the Kitchens. 'Quick! Fetch the Chamberlain at the Ministry of War. He should be in the main chamber!'[64] I said, forgetting proprieties and speaking directly to her. She went to find him but he too had left. I was mortified. Then who should arrive but Sukenari, Chamberlain at the Ministry of Ceremonial, who went round on his own to fill the oil lamps.

Some of the women just sat there gazing at each other in a state of shock. A messenger came from His Majesty. What a dreadful experience it was, I remember. Robes were brought from the imperial storehouse and given to the two women who needed them. Their formal dresses for the New Year's Day celebrations had not been stolen so they put on a brave face, but I shall never forget the sight of them without their clothes. It was frightening but it also had an amusing side to it, although I should never dream of saying so.[65]

*

64 Murasaki is here calling for her younger brother Nobunori, who was always such a disappointment to her. The fact that he fails to turn up is made doubly mortifying when Sukenari, his erstwhile rival for promotion, comes to the rescue.
65 This incident is not mentioned in any other record, although the entries for the latter part of the twelfth month are missing from both Michinaga's diary and the *Shōyūki*. It is

The next day was New Year's Day. We could hardly refrain from discussing last night, although to do so was obviously unlucky. It was also an inauspicious day according to the almanac, so the rice-cake ceremony[66] for the Prince was cancelled. It was in fact the third day of the month before the Prince was taken to see His Majesty.

This year it was Lady Dainagon who was in charge of serving Her Majesty. On the first day she wore a crimson gown with a light purple mantle, a red jacket, and a train of printed silk. For the second day she had a mantle of purple and crimson figured silk, a dark crimson gown of glossy silk, a yellow-green jacket, and a train of variegated colours. For the third day she wore a white mantle of Chinese damask with a red lining, and a dark red jacket of figured silk. As was usually the case, when the gown was dark the lining was a shade paler, and vice versa. Her lined robes were of various colours, pale green, white with a dark-red lining, light yellow, dark yellow, crimson with purple lining, and pale purple lined in white; the effect of these six quite common combinations worn all at one time together with the mantle was perfect.

On the third day Lady Saishō acted as sword bearer, following behind His Excellency, who carried the Prince over to His Majesty's quarters in his arms. She wore one lined crimson robe with seven cuffs which were sewn to the unlined dress beneath, and over that were four more robes of a similar colour with alternating cuffs of three and five layers. Her crimson gown was of thick figured silk with five cuffs. Her mantle was pale purple with a lightly embroidered pattern of oak leaves. Even the stitching was beautifully done. She was also wearing a train with three cuffs, and a red jacket that was embroidered with a

---

possible that burglaries were so commonplace as to be considered unworthy of special notice. Security certainly seems to have been lax. It is also possible that Murasaki had misunderstood the situation. In view of the fact that the best robes were not stolen, we may be dealing with a prank played by some drunken young nobles. Murasaki uses the word *hadakasugata* here, which may mean 'nude' or may simply mean that the women have lost their outer robes: the matter is unclear.

66 This ceremony was carried out for imperial princes and princesses three times during the New Year until they were about four or five years old. Specially made rice cakes were placed on the child's head and spells were cast.

water-chestnut pattern that gave her a rather Chinese look.[07] Her hair
was done up especially for the occasion and she looked and acted
quite perfectly. She is just the right height too, with a full figure, fine
features and a beautiful complexion.

Lady Dainagon is petite, one might almost say small; pale and lovely,
a little plump perhaps, but always very well dressed. Her hair falls
about three inches past her heels and is so luxuriant and kept so
beautifully trimmed there is hardly anyone to match her for elegance.
She has intelligent features and acts in a most charming, graceful
manner.

Lady Senji is also on the small side, but she is very slim. Her hair
falls to about a foot beyond the hem of her robes and not a strand is
ever out of place. She is so infinitely distinguished it quite puts me to
shame, and she has only to put in an appearance to make one feel on
one's guard. Her character and her speech are just what you would
expect of the epitome of a noble lady.

Now if I go on describing people for you in this manner, I am sure I
will get a reputation for being a gossip, especially if it concerns those
close to me.[68] It is too difficult to discuss people I meet every day and I
should avoid commenting on anyone about whom I have second
thoughts.

Lady Saishō – the daughter of Kitano of Third Rank, you know –
has a plump but compact figure and looks very shrewd; she improves
greatly upon further acquaintance. She has a refined air about her and
a most attractive smile plays around the corners of her mouth. The
initial impression she gives is one of correctness and show, but inside
she is in fact lovable and gentle, while in some matters she can still be
positively daunting.

67 This pattern consisted of flat diamond shapes in groups of four, and it was this
geometric effect that struck Murasaki as being rather Chinese.
68 It is at this point that most scholars place the beginning of the so-called 'letter
section', in which Murasaki describes her contemporaries and indulges in some self-
analysis, although the transition from description of event to description of character
has already started a few paragraphs before.

Lady Koshōshō is so indefinably elegant and graceful she reminds one of a weeping willow in spring. She has a lovely figure and a charming manner, but is by nature far too retiring, diffident to the point of being incapable of making up her mind about anything, so naïve that it makes one want to weep. Whenever someone unscrupulous tries to take advantage of her or spreads rumours, she immediately takes it all to heart. She is so vulnerable and so easily dismayed that you would think she were on the point of expiring. I do worry about her.

Miya no Naishi is also very attractive. She is just the right height so that when seated she has a most imposing, stylish air about her. Although not the kind of woman whose attractiveness can be ascribed to any one feature, there is a freshness in her countenance and an air of distinction in her face; the contrast between her pale skin and her black hair sets her apart from the rest. Everything, the shape of her head, her hair, her forehead, surprises with its beauty and yet gives an impression of openness and candour. She acts quite naturally, is kind to others, and never gives the slightest cause for any misgivings. So perfect in whatever she does, she could be a model for all, entirely free from any airs and graces.

Lady Shikibu, her younger sister, is chubby — fat even. She is a pale woman but has delicate, well-formed features. Her hair has a magnificent sheen, but it cannot be that long, for she comes to court with an additional hairpiece attached. I remember her plump little figure as being really most charming. She has pretty eyes and a clear forehead, and is very winsome when she laughs.

Of the younger women, Kodayū and Genshikibu have a reputation of being attractive. Kodayū is petite and very stylish. Her hair is beautiful; it used to be even thicker than it is now and over a foot longer than she was, but recently it has thinned somewhat. Her features show great character and leave a powerful impression. Her looks are impossible to fault. Genshikibu is slim and elegant, the ideal height. She has very fine features and impresses one the more one sees her. Her charm and freshness are just what they should be in 'a girl of good family'.

Kohyōe and Shōni are also very attractive women.

All these ladies-in-waiting must have been approached by senior courtiers at one time or another. If anyone is careless there is no hiding the fact, but somehow, by taking precautions even in private, they do seem to have managed to keep their affairs secret.

Miyagi no Jijū had a delicate kind of beauty. She was very slightly built, the kind of person you wished would always remain a little girl, but she let herself age, became a nun, and we heard no more of her. Her hair used to fall just beyond the hem of her robes, but she cut it boldly on the occasion of her farewell visit to the Palace, I remember. She had beautiful features.

There is one woman called Gosechi no Ben, who, they tell me, was brought up as an adopted daughter by the Middle Counsellor Taira no Korenaka. She has the kind of face you see in paintings, with a very broad forehead and narrow eyes, rather nondescript in fact. She has a pale complexion and beautifully shaped hands and arms, but her hair, which used to be over a foot longer than she was and seemed almost too thick the spring I first saw her, is now extraordinarily thin in places, almost as though someone had cut it deliberately. Even so, it still falls well and reaches to the ground and a little further.

The woman known as Koma had very long hair too. In the past she used to be a marvellous young lady-in-waiting, but now she has become an old stick-in-the-mud and has immured herself at home.

So much for their looks; but their characters – that is a much more difficult matter. We all have our quirks and no one is ever all bad. Then again, it is not possible for everyone to be all things all of the time: attractive, restrained, intelligent, tasteful and trustworthy. We are all different and it is often difficult to know on which aspect to dwell. But I must stop rambling on.

I heard there was a Lady Chūjō serving in the household of the High Priestess of the Kamo Shrines.[69] By chance someone happened to show me in secret a letter which this Lady Chūjō had written. It was dreadfully affected. She seemed to think there was no one in the world as intelligent or discerning as her; everyone else was judged to

---

69 For a discussion of this household see the Introduction, pp. xxi–xxii.

be insensitive and lacking in discrimination. When I saw what she had written, I could hardly contain myself and felt very angry, quite 'worked up' as the saying goes. I know it was a personal letter but she had actually written: 'When it comes to judging poetry, is there anyone who can rival our Princess? She is the only one who could recognize a promising talent nowadays!' There may be some point in what she says, but while she makes such claims for her circle of friends, in fact there are not many poems that her group produces that are of any real merit. Admittedly, it seems to be a very elegant and sophisticated kind of place, but were you to make a comparison, I doubt they would necessarily prove any better than the women I see around me.

They keep themselves very much to themselves. Whenever I have visited them, for it is famous for beautiful moonlit nights, marvellous dawn skies, cherries, and the song of the cuckoo, the High Priestess has always seemed most sensitive. The place has an aura of seclusion and mystery about it, and they have very little to distract them. Rarely are they ever in the rush that we are in whenever Her Majesty visits the Emperor, or when His Excellency decides to come and stay the night. Indeed, the place naturally lends itself to such pleasures, so how could one possibly produce an exchange that offended good taste in the midst of such a striving for the best effects?

If a retiring old fossil like myself were to take service with the High Priestess, I am sure that I would also be able to relax my guard, secure in the knowledge that if I exchanged poems with a man I had not met before I would not automatically be branded a loose woman. I am sure I would absorb the elegance of the place. How much more so if one of our younger women, who have absolutely no drawbacks when it comes to beauty or age, were to put her mind to act seductively and converse by means of poetry; I am convinced that she would compare most favourably.

But here in the Palace there are no other imperial consorts or empresses to keep Her Majesty on her mettle, and there are no ladies-in-waiting in any of the other households who can really challenge us; the result is that all of us, men and women alike, are lacking in any sense of rivalry and simply rest on our laurels. Her Majesty frowns on the slightest hint of seductive behaviour as being the height of frivolity, so anyone who wants to be thought well of takes care never to seem too forward. Of course that is not to say we do not have women among us of quite a different persuasion, women who care nothing for being thought flirtatious and light-hearted and getting a bad name for themselves. The men strike up relationships with this kind of woman because they are such easy game. So they must consider Her Majesty's women either dull or feckless. And as for the upper- and middle-ranking women, they are far too self-satisfied and far too full of themselves. They do nothing to enhance Her Majesty's reputation; in fact they are a disgrace.

Now it may seem that I pretend to know all there is to know about these women, but each one has her own personality and no one is particularly better or worse than anyone else. If they are good in one aspect, they are bad in another, it seems. Mind you, it would, of course, be most improper for the older women to act foolishly at a time when the younger ones themselves are apparently trying to appear serious and dignified; it is just that as a general rule I do wish that they were not quite so stiff.

Her Majesty, although she is so refined, so graceful in all she does, is by nature a little too diffident and will not take the matter up with them. Even were she to do so, she is convinced that there are very few people in this world who can be relied upon with complete confidence. She is right, of course; to do something foolish on an important occasion is worse than just doing things half-heartedly. Once, when she was much younger, Her Majesty heard a lady-in-waiting, who tended to be careless and who thought rather too much of herself on occasions, blurt out some ridiculous things at an important event; it was so dreadfully out of place that she felt deeply shocked. So now she seems to think that the safest policy is to get by in life without a major scandal. I am sure that it is precisely because her women, naïve creatures that they are, have all fitted in so well with her designs that things have turned out as they are.

Her Majesty has gradually matured of late and now understands the ways of the world: that people have their good points and their bad, that they sometimes go to excess and sometimes make mistakes. She is also well aware of the fact that the senior courtiers seem to have become bored with her household, pronouncing it lacking in sparkle.

And yet such reticence is not taken to extremes by all; some women can let themselves go and come out with quite risqué verses. But, although Her Majesty wants the stiff and formal ones to be more lively, and indeed tells them so, their habits are too ingrained. What is more, the young nobles these days are too compliant and act very seriously as long as they are with us. But when they are somewhere like the High Priestess's household they naturally seek to compose all sorts of elegant phrases in praise of the moon or the blossoms, and they say what they think. Here in the Palace, where people traipse in and out day and night and there is little mystery, women who can make the most ordinary conversation sound intriguing or who can compose a passable reply to an interesting poem have become very scarce indeed, or so the men seem to be saying. I have never heard them say this in so many words, however, so I do not know the truth of the matter.

It is ridiculous to respond to someone's overtures with something that causes offence because it has simply been tossed off without due thought. One should take care to give an appropriate response. This is what is meant by the saying 'sensitivity is a precious gift'. Why should self-satisfied smugness be seen as a sign of wisdom? And there again, why should one continually interfere with other people's lives? To be able to adapt to a situation to the correct degree and then to act accordingly seems to be extremely difficult for most people.

For example, whenever the Master of Her Majesty's Household arrives with a message for Her Majesty, the senior women are so helpless and childish that they hardly ever come out to greet him; and when they do, what happens? They seem unable to say anything in the least bit appropriate. It is not that they are at a loss for words, and it is not that they are lacking in intelligence; it is just that they feel so self-conscious and embarrassed that they are afraid of saying something silly, so they refuse to say anything at all and try to make themselves as invisible as possible. Women in other households cannot possibly act in such a manner! Once one has entered this kind of service, even the highest born of ladies learns how to adapt; but our women still act as though they were little girls who had never left home. And as the Master of the Household has made it plain that he objects to being greeted by a woman of a lower rank, there are times when he leaves without seeing anyone; either because the right woman has gone home or because those women who are in their rooms refuse to come out. Other nobles, the kind who often visit Her Majesty with messages, seem to have secret understandings with particular women of their choice and when that woman is absent they simply retire in disappointment. It is hardly surprising that they take every opportunity to complain the place is moribund.

It must be because of all this that the women in the High Priestess's household look down on us. But even so, it makes little sense to ridicule everyone else and claim: 'We are the only ones of note. Everyone else is as good as blind and deaf when it comes to matters of taste.' It is very easy to criticize others but far more difficult to put one's own principles into practice, and it is when one forgets this truth, lauds oneself to the skies, treats everyone else as worthless and generally despises others that one's own character is clearly revealed.

It was a letter I would have loved you to have seen for yourself, but the woman who secretly stole it from its hiding place to show me took it back, I remember – such a pity!

Now someone who did carry on a fascinating correspondence was Izumi Shikibu.[70] She does have a rather unsavoury side to her character but has a talent for tossing off letters with ease and seems to make the most banal statement sound special. Her poems are most interesting. Although her knowledge of the canon and her judgements of other people's poetry leaves something to be desired, she can produce poems at will and always manages to include some clever phrase that catches the attention. Yet when it comes to criticizing or judging the work of others, well, she never really comes up to scratch – the sort of

---

70 Murasaki may have been led on to the subject of Izumi Shikibu because she was Lady Chūjō's aunt, but the main link here is the subject of interesting letters and their authors. Izumi Shikibu entered the service of Shōshi in the late spring of Kankō 6 (1009) and so must have been a companion of Murasaki's for some time, although this passage is written in retrospect.

person who relies on a talent for extemporization, one feels. I cannot think of her as a poet of the highest rank.

The wife of the Governor of Tanba is known to everyone in the service of Her Majesty and His Excellency as Masahira Emon.[71] She may not be a genius but she has great poise and does not feel that she has to compose a poem on everything she sees, merely because she is a poet. From what I have seen, her work is most accomplished, even her occasional verse. People who think so much of themselves that they will, at the drop of a hat, compose lame verses that only just hang together, or produce the most pretentious compositions imaginable, are quite odious and rather pathetic.

Sei Shōnagon, for instance, was dreadfully conceited.[72] She thought herself so clever and littered her writings with Chinese characters; but if you examined them closely, they left a great deal to be desired. Those who think of themselves as being superior to everyone else in this way will inevitably suffer and come to a bad end, and people who have become so precious that they go out of their way to try and be sensitive in the most unpromising situations, trying to capture every moment of interest, however slight, are bound to look ridiculous and superficial. How can the future turn out well for them?

Thus do I criticize others from various angles – but here is one who has survived this far without having achieved anything of note. I have nothing in particular to look forward to in the future that might afford me the slightest consolation, but I am not the kind of person to abandon herself completely to despair. And yet, by the same token, I cannot entirely rid myself of such feelings. On autumn evenings,

71 Otherwise known as Akazome Emon, this is the wife of Ōe no Masahira, who became Governor of Tanba in Kankō 7 (1010).3.30. She had served with Michinaga's wife Rinshi even before her marriage and was the mother of Takachika, who, it will be remembered, read out the passage from the classics at Prince Atsuhira's first bath. She is also reputed to be the author of the *Eiga monogatari.*

72 Sei Shōnagon is the well-known author of the *Pillow Book,* who served Empress Teishi until her mistress died in childbirth in 1000. If she were still alive at this time, and there is no way of telling, she would have been about forty-five.

which positively encourage nostalgia, when I go out to sit on the veranda and gaze, I seem to be always conjuring up visions of the past – 'and did they praise the beauty of this moon of yore?' Knowing full well that I am inviting the kind of misfortune one should avoid, I become uneasy and move inside a little, while still, of course, continuing to recall the past.[73]

And when I play my *koto* rather badly to myself in the cool breeze of the evening, I worry lest someone might hear me and recognize how I am just 'adding to the sadness of it all';[74] how vain and sad of me. So now both my instruments, the one with thirteen strings and the one with six, stand in a miserable, sooty little closet still ready-strung. Through neglect – I forgot, for example, to ask that the bridges be removed on rainy days – they have accumulated dust and lean against a cupboard. Two *biwa* stand on either side, their necks jammed between the cupboard and a pillar.

There is also a pair of larger cupboards crammed to bursting point. One is full of old poems and tales that have become the home for countless insects which scatter in such an unpleasant manner that no one cares to look at them any more; the other is full of Chinese books that have lain unattended ever since he who carefully collected them passed away. Whenever my loneliness threatens to overwhelm me, I take out one or two of them to look at; but my women gather to-gether behind my back. 'It's because she goes on like this that she is so miserable. What kind of lady is it who reads Chinese books?' they whisper. 'In the past it was not even the done thing to read sūtras!' 'Yes,' I feel like replying, 'but I've never met anyone who lived longer just because they believed in superstitions!' But that would be thoughtless of me. There is some truth in what they say.

73 The rhythm here suggests a direct quote from a poem, but no satisfactory source has been identified. Misfortune will come from looking too long and too often at the moon and hence identifying with it; this was said to promote nostalgia, grief and premature ageing.

74 A reference to Poem 985 in the *Kokinshū* by Yoshimine no Munesada (Bishop Henjō): 'While on his way to Nara he heard a woman playing a *koto* in a dilapidated house. He wrote this poem and sent it in: *It seemed to be a dwelling where you might expect someone dejected to be living; and now I hear the sound of a koto that adds to the sadness of it all.*'

Each one of us is quite different. Some are confident, open and forthcoming. Others are born pessimists, amused by nothing, the kind who search through old letters, carry out penances, intone sūtras without end, and clack their beads, all of which makes one feel uncomfortable. So I hesitate to do even those things I should be able to do quite freely, only too aware of my own servants' prying eyes. How much more so at court, where I have many things I would like to say but always think the better of it, because there would be no point in explaining to people who would never understand. I cannot be bothered to discuss matters in front of those women who continually carp and are so full of themselves: it would only cause trouble. It is so rare to find someone of true understanding; for the most part they judge purely by their own standards and ignore everyone else.

So all they see of me is a façade. There are times when I am forced to sit with them and on such occasions I simply ignore their petty criticisms, not because I am particularly shy but because I consider it pointless. As a result, they now look upon me as a dullard.

'Well, we never expected this!' they all say. 'No one liked her. They all said she was pretentious, awkward, difficult to approach, prickly, too fond of her tales, haughty, prone to versifying, disdainful, cantankerous and scornful; but when you meet her, she is strangely meek, a completely different person altogether!'

How embarrassing! Do they really look upon me as such a dull thing, I wonder? But I am what I am. Her Majesty has also remarked more than once that she had thought I was not the kind of person with whom she could ever relax, but that I have now become closer to her than any of the others. I am so perverse and standoffish. If only I can avoid putting off those for whom I have a genuine regard.

To be pleasant, gentle, calm and self-possessed: this is the basis of good taste and charm in a woman. No matter how amorous or passionate you may be, as long as you are straightforward and refrain from causing others embarrassment, no one will mind. But women who are too vain and act pretentiously, to the extent that they make others feel uncomfortable, will themselves become the object of attention; and once that happens, people will always find fault with whatever they say or do: whether it be how they enter a room, how they sit down, how they stand up or how they take their leave. Those who end up contradicting themselves and those who disparage their companions are also carefully watched and listened to all the more. As long as you are free from such faults, people will surely refrain from listening to tittle-tattle and will want to show you sympathy, if only for the sake of politeness.

I am of the opinion that when you intentionally cause hurt to another, or indeed if you do ill through mere thoughtless behaviour, you fully deserve to be censured in public. Some people are so good-natured that they can still care for those who despise them, but I myself find it very difficult. Did the Buddha himself in all his compassion ever preach that one should simply ignore those who slander the Three Treasures?[75] How in this sullied world of ours can those who are hard done by be expected not to reciprocate in kind? And yet people react in very different ways. Some glare at each other face to face and fling abuse in an attempt to gain the upper hand; others hide their true intent and appear quite friendly on the surface – thus are true natures revealed.

There is a woman called Saemon no Naishi who, for some strange reason, took a dislike to me. I heard all sorts of malicious, unfounded rumours about myself. His Majesty was listening to someone reading the *Tale of Genji* aloud. 'She must have read the *Chronicles of Japan*!' he said. 'She seems very learned.' Saemon no Naishi suddenly jumped to conclusions and spread it abroad among the senior courtiers that I was flaunting my learning. She gave me the nickname Lady Chronicle. How very comical! Would I, who hesitate to show my learning even in front of my own servants at home, ever dream of doing so at court?

When my brother, Secretary at the Ministry of Ceremonial,[76] was a

75 The Three Treasures without which the teachings would not survive were the Buddha himself, the Buddhist Law, and the community of monks who preserved that law. Slander of these three treasures was one of the gravest of offences.

76 Murasaki's brother was given the title Secretary at the Ministry of War earlier in the diary. When he changed is not known. It is possible that 'Ministry of Ceremonial' (Shikibu) is a simple mistake, which may have arisen because Murasaki's father, who is mentioned later in this same passage, did at one stage hold this post.

young boy learning the Chinese classics, I was in the habit of listening with him and I became unusually proficient at understanding those passages that he found too difficult to grasp and memorize. Father, a most learned man, was always regretting the fact: 'Just my luck!' he would say. 'What a pity she was not born a man!' But then I gradually realized that people were saying 'It's bad enough when a man flaunts his Chinese learning; she will come to no good,' and since then I have avoided writing the simplest character. My handwriting is appalling. And as for those 'classics' or whatever they are that I used to read, I gave them up entirely. Yet still I kept on hearing these remarks; so in the end, worried what people would think if they heard such rumours, I pretended to be incapable of reading even the inscriptions on the screens. Then Her Majesty asked me to read with her here and there from the *Collected Works* of Po Chü-i,[77] and, because she evinced a desire to know more about such things, to keep it secret we carefully chose times when the other women would not be present, and, from the summer before last, I started giving her informal lessons on the two volumes of 'New Ballads'. I hid this fact from others, as did Her Majesty, but somehow both His Excellency and His Majesty got wind of it and they had some beautiful copies made of various Chinese books, which His Excellency then presented to her. That gossip Saemon no Naishi could never have found out that Her Majesty had actually asked me to study with her, for had she done so, I would never have heard the last of it. Ah, what a prattling, tiresome world it is!

Why should I hesitate to say what I want to? Whatever others might say, I intend to immerse myself in reading sūtras for Amida Buddha. Since I have lost what little attachment I ever had for the pains that life has to offer, you might expect me to become a nun without delay. But even supposing I were to commit myself and turn my back on the world, I am certain there would be moments of irresolution before

**77** Po Chü-i (772–846) was a T'ang dynasty Chinese poet who had the distinction of being well-known and read in Japan during his own lifetime. In Murasaki's time his work still formed the foundation of a courtier's knowledge of Chinese poetry.

Amida came for me riding on his clouds. And thus I hesitate. I know the time is opportune. If I get much older my eyesight will surely weaken, I shall be unable to read sūtras, and my spirits will fail. It may seem that I am merely going through the motions of being a true believer, but I assure you that now I think of little else. But then someone with as much to atone for as myself may not qualify for salvation; there are so many things that serve to remind one of the transgressions of a former existence.[78] Everything conspires to make me unhappy.

I want to reveal all to you, the good and the bad, worldly matters and private sorrows, things that I cannot really go on discussing in this letter. But, even though one may be thinking about and describing someone objectionable, should one really go on like this, I wonder? But you must find life irksome at times. I know I do, as you can see. Write to me with your own thoughts – no matter if you have less to say than all my useless prattle, I would love to hear from you. Mind you, if this letter ever got into the wrong hands it would be a disaster – there are ears everywhere.

I have recently torn up and burned most of my old letters and papers. I used the rest to make dolls' houses this last spring and since then no one has written. I feel I should not use new paper, so I am afraid this will look very shabby. It is not through lack of care; quite the opposite.

Please return this as soon as you have read it. There may be parts that are difficult to read and places where I have left out a word or two, but just disregard them and read it through. So you see – I still fret over what others think of me, and, if I had to sum up my position, I would have to admit that I still retain a deep sense of attachment to this world. But what can I do about it?

*

78 Murasaki may be thinking of the fact that she was born a woman and so might well have to go through at least one further rebirth as a man. In Early Buddhism the female state was a major handicap to enlightenment, although by Murasaki's time in Japan textual 'proof' was available, particularly in the *Lotus Sūtra*, that enlightenment was more or less attainable by women.

Her Majesty went over to the Dedication Hall just before dawn on the eleventh.[79] Her Excellency was with her in the carriage and the ladies-in-waiting crossed by boat. I went over much later in the evening. They were in the process of distributing lotus petals and intoning the Great Confession exactly as it is performed at Hieizan and the Miidera. The nobles had been amusing themselves painting small white pagodas on as many petals as they could, but now most of them had left and only a few remained.

In the early morning each of the preachers – there were twenty – gave a little congratulatory sermon in honour of Her Majesty; a number of them caused some amusement because they kept on interrupting each other and getting tongue-tied.

When it was all over, the senior courtiers took the boats and rowed out together on to the lake to play music. On the eastern veranda of the Hall in front of the open side door sat Tadanobu, the Master of Her Majesty's Household. He was leaning against the railings of the steps that ran down to the water's edge. When His Excellency went inside to talk to Her Majesty for a moment, Tadanobu took the opportunity to exchange a few words with Lady Saishō; what with him outside the screens and her inside trying not to appear too intimate in front of Her Majesty, it was quite a performance.

A hazy moon emerged. It was refreshing and pleasant to hear His Excellency's sons all in the one boat singing songs in the modern style, but it was amusing to see Masamitsu, Minister of the Treasury, who had got in with them in all seriousness, now sitting there meekly with his back to us, not unnaturally loath to take part. The women behind the screens laughed softly. 'And in the boat he seems to feel his age,' I said.

The Master of the Household must have heard me.

'Hsu Fu and Wen Ch'eng were empty braggarts,' he murmured. I was most impressed.[80]

---

79 Here there is a definite break. One theory has it that this passage actually predates the beginning of the present diary. See the Introduction (p. xlvi) for further discussion.
80 Murasaki has just quoted a line from one of Po Chü-i's New Ballads entitled 'The Ocean Wide', which is concerned with the search for a magic elixir from the fabled mountainous isle of Peng-lai (Jp.: Hōrai), which was mentioned earlier with reference to a pattern. Tadanobu immediately caps it with the next line from the poem.

'And the duckweed upon the lake,' came the words of the song; there was also a flute accompanying them which somehow intensified the coolness of the dawn breeze. The most insignificant thing can have its season.

His Excellency happened to see that Her Majesty had the *Tale of Genji* with her. Out came the usual comments, and then on a piece of paper that held some plums he wrote:

> She is known for her tartness
> So I am sure that no one seeing her
> Could pass without a taste

and he handed it to me.

> She is a fruit that no one has yet tasted –
> Who then can smack his lips and talk of tartness?[81]

'I am shocked,' I replied.

One night as I lay asleep in a room in the corridor, there came the sound of someone tapping at the door. I was so frightened that I kept quiet for the rest of the night. Early next morning I received:

> Crying crying all night long
> More constant than the water rail
> In vain did I tap at your door.

To which I replied:

> The water rail was indeed insistent;
> But had I opened up, come dawn,
> I may well have had bitter regrets.[82]

\*

81 Both of these poems revolve round a pun on the word *suki*, which can mean either 'tart', in reference to the fruit, or 'amorous', in reference to a man or woman.
82 The cry of the water rail was thought to sound like tapping on wood, hence the conventional association of this bird with the visit of a lover.

This year, each day for the first three days of the New Year, the senior ladies-in-waiting all accompanied the imperial princes to the Palace for the ceremony of the rice cakes.[83] Yorimichi, Commander of the Gate Guards of the Left, carried the boys in his arms, and His Excellency himself passed on the rice cakes, presenting them to His Majesty, who in turn stood facing the eastern doors of the Two-Bay Room and placed the cakes on their heads. The processions there and back were marvellous spectacles. Her Majesty did not attend.

On New Year's Day this year Lady Saishō was in charge of serving the meal. As usual she was most tastefully dressed and looked very attractive. Two maids, Takumi and Hyōgo, were also present; but with her hair done up Lady Saishō really stood out, poor thing.

The woman in charge of the spiced wine, Lady Fuya, was officious and overbearing. The distribution of the ointment was carried out as usual.

On the second day, Her Majesty's formal banquet was cancelled, so the guests for the informal gathering were accommodated as usual by opening up the eastern gallery. The nobles sat facing each other in two rows. Present were Mentor and Major Counsellor Michitsuna, Major Captain of the Right Sanesuke, Master of Her Majesty's Household Tadanobu, Shijō Major Counsellor Kintō, Middle Counsellor Elect Takaie, Gentleman-in-waiting and Middle Counsellor Yukinari, Commander of the Gate Guards of the Left Yorimichi, Adviser Arikuni, Minister of the Treasury Masamitsu, Commander of the Military Guards of the Left Sanenari and Adviser Minamoto no Yorisada. Middle Counsellor Minamoto no Toshikata, Commander of the Gate

83 At this point all extant manuscripts carry the following annotation, thought to be by the scholar and poet Fujiwara no Teika (1162–1241): 'In Kankō 6 (1009).10.4 the Ichijō Palace burned down. On the 19th the Emperor moved to the Biwa mansion belonging to Minister of the Left Michinaga. On the 25th of the eleventh month the third prince was born, the Empress returning to the Palace on the 26th of the twelfth month.' This means that the word 'Palace' here and in what follows is in fact Michinaga's Biwa mansion. The court did not finally return to the palace at Ichijō until Kankō 7 (1010).11.28. We are now at the beginning of 1010. There are now two princes: Atsuhira and his younger brother Atsunaga, born Kankō 6 (1009).11.25. The annotation says 'third prince' because it is also counting the son born to the Emperor's first consort, Teishi.

Guards of the Right Yasuhira, and Advisers of the Left Tsunefusa and of the Right Kanetaka sat on the veranda outside at the head of the senior courtiers.

His Excellency picked up the elder prince in his arms and brought him out, making him greet the guests with a word and generally fussing over him. Then, turning to Her Excellency, he said 'Let me take the younger one now.' At this the elder boy grew very jealous and wailed in protest, so that His Excellency had to fuss over him again to placate him. Major Captain Sanesuke and a few others found this very amusing.

Then they all went to pay their respects to His Majesty, who came out to meet them in the Senior Courtier's Hall. There was music and His Excellency started drinking as usual. Foreseeing trouble, I made myself inconspicuous, but to no avail.

'Why!' he cried in a vexed tone. 'Why, when I asked him to attend the concert, did your papa scuttle off like that? Sulking is he?'

Then he pressed me further.

'Give me a poem good enough to compensate!' he said. 'For your father. It's the first day of the Rat. Come on, come on!'

But it would have been out of place for me to have done so.

He did not seem to be very drunk; in fact he looked rather handsome and attractive, standing there in the light of the torches.

'I was worried to see Her Majesty alone without any children for so long,' he said. 'But now they seem to be everywhere! How marvellous!' And with that he went over to take a peek at the princes, who were by now both asleep.

'If there were no small pines in the fields,'[84] he murmured to himself. Such a fitting reference, I felt; far better than any new poem of mine could have ever been. I was most impressed.

Next day, sometime late in the afternoon, the sky suddenly became very misty, but the eaves were built so close together that all I could see of it was a patch just above the roof of the corridor opposite. I

---

84 An apposite quote from a poem attributed to Mibu no Tadamine: '*If there were no small pines in the fields on the day of the Rat, then what could we pick as a sign of future fortunes?*' (*Shūishū*, Poem 23). It was the custom to go out into the fields and pick young shoots and pine seedlings on the first day of the Rat every year.

happened to be with Lady Nakatsukasa and I told her how moved I had been by His Excellency's impromptu reference of the previous evening. What a sensitive, intelligent creature she is!

I went home for a short while but then returned for the fiftieth-day celebrations for the Second Prince, which took place on the fifteenth of the first month. I arrived at the Palace just before dawn, but Lady Koshōshō came much later when it was fully light, which was rather embarrassing for her. As usual we shared. We had made our two adjacent rooms into one, using it even when one of us was away at home. When we were both serving at court hanging curtains were all that separated us. His Excellency was amused.

'What happens when you entertain someone the other one does not know?' he said. A tasteless remark. In any case, we are both very close to each other, so there would be no problem.

About midday, we went to attend to Her Majesty. Lady Koshōshō wore a red jacket over robes of white figured silk lined with red, with the usual printed train. I wore a jacket with cuffs of white lined with pale green over robes of crimson lined with purple, and pale green lined with a slightly darker green, together with a printed train; it was all a bit extravagant and so youthful looking that I should have exchanged my dress for hers. Seventeen women from the Palace were also in attendance on Her Majesty. Lady Tachibana was in charge of serving the Second Prince's meal. The women whose job it was to pass in the food were Kodayū and Genshikibu, who sat outside by the veranda, and Lady Koshōshō, who sat inside.

The Emperor and Her Majesty were in their respective curtained daises. They were as resplendent as the morning sun, dazzling in their brilliance. The Emperor wore ordinary court dress with wide trousers drawn in at the ankles. Her Majesty wore her usual unlined crimson dress, robes of crimson lined with purple, pale green lined with darker green, white lined with pale green, and yellow lined with darker yellow. Her mantle was of light purple figured silk, over which she wore an informal outer robe that was white lined with pale green. The pattern and colours were most unusual and up-to-date. Since it was too exposed out there in front, I made myself inconspicuous in the back.

Lady Nakatsukasa, carrying the little prince in her arms, came out from between the two daises and brought him into the southern part of the hall. In no way formal or imposing, she has, however, composure and dignity, and looks intelligent; a born teacher. She wore light purple robes of figured silk, a mantle of plain green, and a jacket with cuffs of white lined with dark red.

That day all the women had done their utmost to dress well, but, as luck would have it, two of them showed a want of taste when it came to the colour combinations at their sleeves, and as they served the food they came into full view of the nobles and senior courtiers. Later, it seemed that Lady Saishō and the others had been mortified; but it was not such a terrible mistake – it was just that the combinations were rather uninspiring. Kodayū had worn an unlined crimson dress with robes of five layers in differing shades of crimson with purple linings. Her jacket was white lined with deep red. It seems that Genshikibu had worn robes of deep crimson lined with purple and a damask mantle of crimson lined again with purple. Was it because her jacket was not of figured silk? But that would be ridiculous.[85] The slightest mistake in a formal setting should indeed be the subject of censure, but there is no sense in criticizing the material itself.

After the ceremony of touching the rice cake to the children's lips was over and the trays were removed, the gallery blinds were rolled up. Then the women from the Palace moved over to sit in close ranks to the west of the dais, where His Majesty usually sat. Lady Tachibana was there together with a number of assistant handmaids.

As for Her Majesty's women, the younger ones sat out on the veranda and the senior ones sat in the eastern gallery, where the screens on the south side had been replaced by blinds. I went to where Lady Dainagon and Lady Koshōshō were sitting in the narrow space between Her Majesty's dais and the eastern gallery and watched the proceedings from there.

**85** Murasaki apparently thought that Kodayū's colour sense was at fault but she is unsure as to why Genshikibu was being criticized. Genshikibu was not of a high enough rank to wear the 'forbidden colours' and so could not have worn a mantle in figured silk even if she had wished to.

His Majesty moved to his seat and the food was brought in. It was so beautifully arranged I cannot find words to describe it. Out on the southern veranda facing north and ranked from west to east sat the nobles. The three Great Ministers of the Left, Right and Centre were there, as were Michitsuna, the Crown Prince's Mentor, Tadanobu, Master of Her Majesty's Household, and Kintō, Shijō Major Counsellor. From where I was sitting I could not see the others below them.

There was music. The senior courtiers sat in the corridor at the south-eastern corner of the wing and those of lower rank sat where they usually did on these occasions, in the garden – men like Kagemasa, Korekaze, Yukiyoshi and Tōmasa.

Up in the gallery Kintō marked time with the clappers. Chamberlain Michikata played the *biwa*, ★★★★[86] the *koto*, and Adviser Tsunefusa the hand pipes. They sang 'Ah how sacred!' 'Mushiroda' and 'These Halls', all to the *sōjō* mode.[87] For music they chose the last two movements of the 'Dance of the Kalavinka Bird'. Down in the garden flues were playing in accompaniment. The one who made a mistake in marking time for the songs and who was scolded for it was the Governor of Ise. The Minister of the Right, Akimitsu, became somewhat over-enthusiastic about the *koto* playing and started to play pranks which ended up with his making a dreadful fool of himself.[88] We all shuddered to watch. I saw His Excellency present the Emperor with a box containing the famous flute Hafutatsu.[89]

---

86 There is a lacuna at this point in the text and one can only guess at who is meant.

87 The *sōjō* mode, with a scale of g a b d e, was the third of the six basic *gagaku* modes. The three songs are *saibara*, old folk songs incorporated into court music.

88 Michinaga's diary for this day reads: 'Showers. In the evening the sky cleared and the moon was bright. While the music was being played the guards provided torches, but the flares in the garden were extinguished so that we could see the moon. When it was all over we went inside. Minister of the Right Akimitsu caught sight of the Emperor's meal and tried to pick up a bowl and some food which was piled in between the ornamental cranes. He tipped the whole tray over. Everyone was most shocked. The cranes should not have been touched! What a blunderer! How stupid of him!'

89 This was the name of a famous flute that Michinaga had been given just a few days previously by Retired Emperor Kazan. The significance of the name ('two teeth'?) is not known, but prized instruments and utensils were often given nicknames that reflected some aspect of their origin.

# APPENDIX I
# GROUND-PLANS
# AND MAP

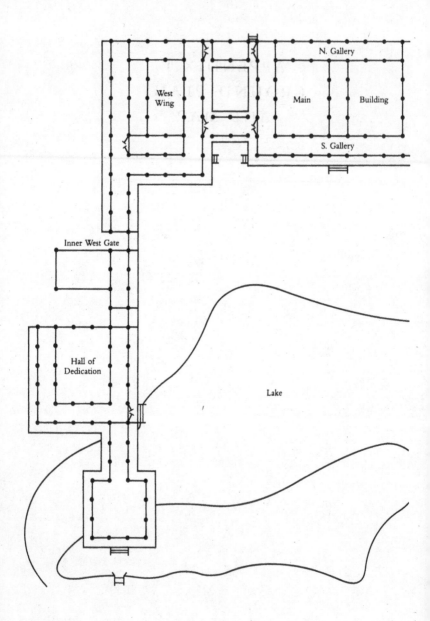

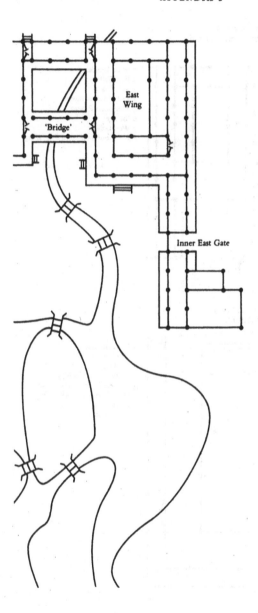

GROUND-PLAN 2
Tsuchimikado Mansion – Detail

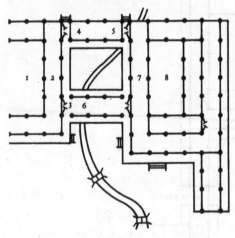

1 Main Building
2 East Gallery
3 Side Doors
4 Lady Saishō's Room
5 Murasaki's Room
6 'Bridge'
7 West Gallery
8 Religious Service in East Wing

GROUND-PLAN 3
Birth of Atsuhira

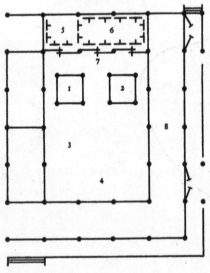

1 Normal Dais
2 White Dais
3 Mediums
4 Archbishops and Bishops
5 Murasaki and Ladies-in-Waiting
6 Her Majesty in Back Gallery
7 Crush of Forty Women
8 Palace Ladies

## GROUND-PLAN 4
### The First Bath

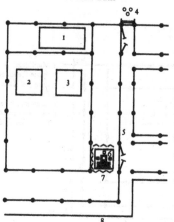

1 Her Majesty
2 Normal Dais
3 White Dais
4 Tubs and Stand
5 Water Handed Through Blinds Here
6 Bath with Pitchers
7 Screens
8 Readers

## GROUND-PLAN 5
### Fifth-Day Celebrations

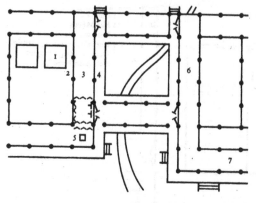

1 Her Majesty's Dais
2 Eight Ladies-in-Waiting
3 Thirty or More Women
4 Menials and Serving Girls
5 Double Screens with Food
6 Senior Courtiers
7 Lesser Courtiers

### GROUND-PLAN 6
#### The Imperial Visit

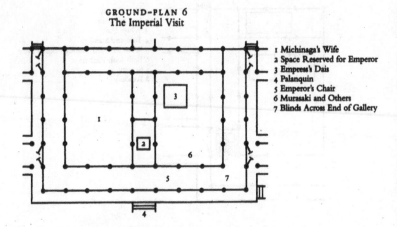

1 Michinaga's Wife
2 Space Reserved for Emperor
3 Empress's Dais
4 Palanquin
5 Emperor's Chair
6 Murasaki and Others
7 Blinds Across End of Gallery

### GROUND-PLAN 7
#### Fiftieth-Day Celebrations

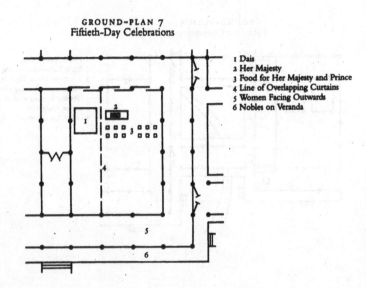

1 Dais
2 Her Majesty
3 Food for Her Majesty and Prince
4 Line of Overlapping Curtains
5 Women Facing Outwards
6 Nobles on Veranda

GROUND-PLAN 8
Ichijō Palace

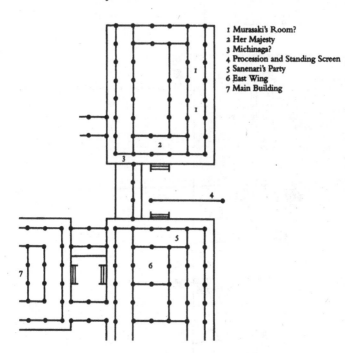

1 Murasaki's Room?
2 Her Majesty
3 Michinaga?
4 Procession and Standing Screen
5 Sanenari's Party
6 East Wing
7 Main Building

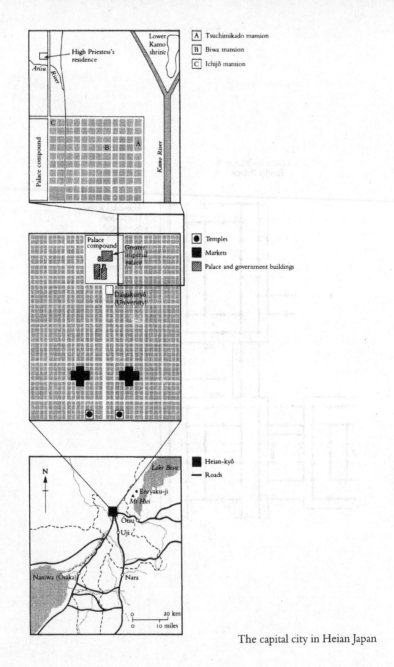

A Tsuchimikado mansion
B Biwa mansion
C Ichijō mansion

Temples
Markets
Palace and government buildings

Heian-kyō
Roads

The capital city in Heian Japan

# APPENDIX 2
# ADDITIONAL SOURCES

In part because the birth of Prince Atsuhira was such an important event for Michinaga and his branch of the Fujiwara family, there are a number of extant records in Sino-Japanese that cover similar ground to Murasaki's diary. Not only do they provide a background of factual details which often help us to understand her diary correctly, but they also reveal the different perspective that men writing in Sino-Japanese and women writing in pure Japanese brought to their description of events at court. Translated here are a few relevant sections from two of the three anonymous descriptions, *Fuchiki A* and *B*, taken from a manuscript in the Imperial Library entitled *Gosanki burui* ('Classified Records of Imperial Births'), and from Fujiwara no Sanesuke's diary the *Shōyūki*. Except for *Fuchiki B* these extracts cover the main events during the ninth month of 1008.

## (a) Fuchiki A

(Probably of much later provenance and influenced by Murasaki's diary)

Kankō 5 (1008).8.11. The furnishings for Her Majesty's lying-in were brought over from the Palace. One dais made of white wood with damask curtains and five supports each painted white; three pairs of five-foot screens and three pairs of four-foot screens made of white damask backed with black, black and white design on the borders, and the usual gold fittings; three pairs of four-foot curtain frames and two pairs of three-foot frames with damask curtains; thirteen thick mats with borders of white damask; everything else had damask edging too; one extra cover edged with figured silk. Everything packed in black lacquer boxes and containers.

9.11. Fair. Her Majesty gave birth to a son in the Tsuchimikado mansion about midday. Yorisada arrived outside the Palace gates and had a Chamberlain announce the good news to the Emperor. Then he was ordered to present the sword to Her Majesty. He returned to the mansion, stood outside the centre west gate, and had Tsunefusa announce him. Then he proceeded to where mats had already been laid down on the veranda in front of the blinds along the southern gallery. Michinaga talked to him for a moment and then presented him with a set of women's robes. He went back down the southern steps, bowed for a second time, and returned to the Palace; his attendant received two rolls of silk. His report was sent in to the Emperor and received by the Middle Counsellor Elect just as in the case of the messenger to Ise. The first bath was held at about eight that evening. Two clerks and four scribes wearing white vestments carried in the bathtub and various other utensils, bringing them to Her Majesty along the east 'bridge'. Then Doctor of Letters Hironari, who was carrying the opening passage from the *Records of the Grand Historian*, led in twenty bowmen, ten of Fifth Rank and ten of Sixth. They came in from the same direction, and stood facing north, ranked west to east. Hironari started his reading. When he had finished, they all left. The evening bath was held late at night. Doctor of Confucianism Munetoki did the reading (from the *Classic of Filial Piety*). Takachika was also a reader.

Events on the third day. Her Majesty's Household arranged the celebrations; six trays with silver utensils. The nobles, senior courtiers, and masters all had a banquet. There was food for the retainers and also betting. The baby prince was given a pair of clothes chests made of nettle-tree wood with silver clasps and set on a Chinese table covered with a cloth.

Events on the fifth day. Michinaga arranged the celebrations. Six trays with silver utensils. Two cabinets were put out on the veranda and the food was placed in them. There was a banquet, food for the retainers, and gifts, a woman's wardrobe for the nobles, robes for the retainers. Today those with the rank of scholar and student in the Kangakuin came in procession to present their congratulations. Scholar Tokitaka was also present to bow and receive a gift.

Seventh day. Fair. The seventh night after the birth. Celebration held under the auspices of the Palace. There was food, six trays made of nettle-tree wood with mother-of-pearl inlay. The surface was embossed in places. The cloth too was intricately woven and inset with ivory. The food boxes, chopstick-rests, sake cups, and bowls had all been prepared by the Imperial Table Office. There were twenty-five sets of robes, 120 rolls of silk, 300 lbs of cotton, and 500 pieces of Shinano cloth, all packed in ten large boxes; fifty banquet settings from the Bureau of Palace Storehouses, fifty meals from the Granary, and twenty meals for retainers from the Kitchens of the women's quarters at the Palace. The Imperial messenger Michimasa, together with an accountant, was given a gift and reported back to the Palace. Officials from the Imperial Table Office came to the bottom of the steps, where women servants took the food and presented it. That done, the officials were given one roll of silk each. Akimitsu and the other nobles held a banquet in the east wing; they sat in the southern gallery, facing north and ranked west to east. The three Doctors of Letters were also present. Then the nobles went over the 'bridge', sang congratulatory songs and received presents in return. Ministers received women's dresses; Tadanobu a women's wardrobe and baby clothes; those between the rank of Major Counsellor and Adviser women's dresses, one robe of damask, and baby clothes; senior courtiers and masters one roll of silk each, except that two of the more important men had baby clothes in addition.

## (b) Fuchiki B

Kankō 5 (1008).9.11. Fair. Her Majesty gave birth in the Jōtōmon'in; the north gallery of the central chamber was chosen as the place of birth. She had been having contractions since dawn on the tenth, so at about four that morning they moved away the normal dais and set up one made of white wood with 'cicada-wing' curtains and gauze ribbons; there were 12 screens of white damask and the dais itself was also white with gauze curtains and ribbons. They also provided mats with white borders. The dais, thick mats, etc., had previously been arranged by Michikata and Sadasuke on imperial order. One day last month, the eighth, Sadasuke, acting as imperial envoy, had brought them over from the Palace. He was given a gift of a set of women's dresses. The accountant Tahiji no Tokimasa received women's robes, and the attendant from the Secretariat one roll of white silk. The other attendants received one roll of red silk each. Then the rice for casting was prepared in six white tubs, arranged by the Household. Meanwhile many prayers were offered up. About noon the baby was safely delivered. They called up the Yin-Yang diviners, Kamo no Mitsuhide, Abe no Yoshihira and Agata no Tomohira, who were given gifts, three rolls for Fourth Rank, two for Fifth Rank. They were asked to calculate the calendar of events for the first giving of the breast and other ceremonies. The duty of giving the breast was given to Tachibana no Tokushi because she had been the Emperor's wet nurse. She received a woman's wardrobe as a gift. The three readers were named: Doctor of Confucianism Nakahara no Munetoki, Doctor of Letters Fujiwara no Hironari and Ōe no Takachika. There were twenty bowmen; ten of Fifth Rank, Ōe no Kagemasa, Ki no Tadamichi, Taira no Masayoshi, Fujiwara no Sueyori, Fujiwara no Takanao, Sugawara no Tamemasa, Fujiwara no Tomomitsu,

Minamoto no Nagamitsu, Minamoto no Tadataka, Fujiwara no Sadasuke; and ten of Sixth Rank, Takashina no Arihira, Minamoto no Tameyoshi, Fujiwara no Naganobu, Fujiwara no Chikanori, Fujiwara no Ienari, Fujiwara no Mochi-michi, Takashina no Yorihira, Fujiwara no Akinobu, Minamoto no Yorikuni, Tachibana no Yoshimichi, all dressed in white.

Minamoto no Yorisada then brought in the sword; it was wrapped in a brocade cover and carried by an attendant. One thick mat with black and white patterned borders, and another rush mat were laid out on the southern veranda of the main building to mark where he should sit. Michinaga took the sword. Tadanobu passed the gift, a set of women's robes, to Michinaga, who then gave them to Yorisada. Yorisada then went down the southern steps, bowed once more, and left. His attendant received two rolls of silk. At about the same time the order was given for the bathtub and other necessities to be constructed; Her Majesty's Household took charge of this. A pair of tubs with stands; sixteen pitchers and two tables, eight on each table, all covered with white material; two low benches, each with a small mat and one side-table; six pails, two large, four small, each covered in white silk; six ladles, two large, four small. At about five in the afternoon in accordance with the diviners' calcula-tions flowing water was drawn from the north north-west by one clerk, one scribe and two servants, all dressed in white vestments.

The first bath started about eight. The bath itself was on the eastern ver-anda of the main building. First they laid a covering of hand-made cloth, with a second layer of white silk over it, each piece being about fifteen feet in length. Two clerks, Marube no Kaneyoshi and Takeda no Toshinari, two scribes, Koremune no Shigekane and Kawabe no Takesuke, and two attend-ants from the Household, Hasebe no Nagamori and Ban no Yoshikane, each wearing white vestments over their usual dress, brought the water from the small steps in the north-east corner of the main building. The two attendants then carried it up and passed it in to the women. Meanwhile officials from the Bureau of Grounds stood in attendance, carrying torches. Archbishop Shōsan came in response to a request and blessed the bath. Fujiwara no Hōshi was in charge of the ceremony, aided by Minamoto no Renshi, daughter of Suke-yoshi. Then came the reading. It was Hironari reading the *Classic of Filial Piety*; Doctor of Letters read first. He led the bowmen in and lined them up in the southern garden. The reader stood in front and the bowmen stood in two rows behind him, ranked from the front, west to east. When it was finished they left.

The food was brought forward: six trays with plates and food boxes, all of white wood; various other utensils; same for the next seven days. Six girls, each dressed in white jackets and trains, served the meal. About midnight the evening bath was performed, the ceremony being the same as before. The reader was Hironari. While it was in progress Michinaga and the other nobles were on the east 'bridge', and the senior courtiers and Masters of the Household were on the veranda of the east wing. Her Majesty's Household provided congee and other refreshments for everyone; same for the next seven days.

9.12. Fair. The reader at the morning bath was Munetoki, reading from the *Doctrine of the Mean*. At the evening bath the reader was Takachika, reading from the opening passage of the *Records of the Grand Historian*. The ceremony was the same as the previous day.

9.13. Fair. At the morning bath the reader was Hironari, and in the evening Munetoki read the 'Ta Ming' from the *Book of Songs*. Ceremony as before. That evening Her Majesty's Household arranged the food, the banquet, tables, thirty meals for retainers, and then the betting. Four-foot screens of white damask were set up in the western gallery of the east wing for the nobles, who sat facing each other, ranked north to south. Similar screens were erected in the southern gallery for the senior courtiers, who faced each other, ranked west to east. The Masters of the Household sat in the eastern extension, each with his own table. About eight in the evening everyone took his place: Fujiwara no Michitsuna, Fujiwara no Sanesuke, Fujiwara no Yasutada, Fujiwara no Tadanobu, Fujiwara no Kintō, Fujiwara no Takaie, Fujiwara no Tokimitsu, Minamoto no Toshikata, Fujiwara no Tadasuke, Fujiwara no Arikuni, Fujiwara no Yukinari, Taira no Chikanobu, Fujiwara no Yasuhira, Fujiwara no Kanetaka, Minamoto no Tsunefusa, Fujiwara no Masamitsu, Fujiwara no Yorimichi, Minamoto no Norisada and Fujiwara no Sanenari. Officials from the Bureau of Grounds stood in attendance, carrying torches. After the sake cup had been passed around for the second time, the students from the Kangakuin, led by the scholar Tokitaka, entered in procession. Tachibana no Tameyoshi showed the list of participants to the Master of the Household and then had it presented to Her Majesty. Once the order came that it had been accepted, they all lined up in the southern garden, bowed once again, and retired. Gifts were given according to rank. The scholar got one set of robes, the students, etc., a roll of silk each, clerks four pieces of Shinano cloth each, and the others two pieces of linen. About ten in the evening the food was served: six trays made from young aloes-wood with mother-of-pearl inlay; embroidered gauze coverlets and other material; food boxes, plates, cruet-sets, chopstick-rests, etc., all made of silver. The Master of Fifth Rank and others carried the food in and handed it to the serving girls, who in turn passed it to the ladies-in-waiting standing outside the eastern side door of the main building. Tadanobu was in charge. The baby's clothes were in four caskets. Two contained three sets of clothes in white figured silk and three sets in damask. The boxes were of young aloes-wood and had a river scene depicted on them, silver for the river, aloes-wood for the stones; they were covered with gauze and placed on a table of aloes-wood inlaid with mother-of-pearl. There were other coverlets. This was all Toshikata's offering. The other offering was by Sanenari: two caskets with bedding for the baby, two sets in damask, one in plain silk. The caskets were embossed with a silver wave design, were backed with aloes-wood, and had gauze covers. These clothes were carried by senior courtiers of Fourth Rank and given to the ladies-in-waiting. Then the nobles and everyone else started betting. Finally came the ceremony of parading the food, which was carried out by seven men of Fifth Rank: Ki no Arichika, Minamoto no Masayuki, Fujiwara no Kinnori, Taira no Tomotaka, Taira no Nakamasa, Minamoto no Nobuchika, Fujiwara no Yorinobu. Ōe no Kiyomichi stood on top of the southern steps acting as prompter. The leader repeated the auspicious phrases three times and then the nobles all withdrew.

1008.9.14. Fair. About midday the morning bath was performed. Takachika read 'The Hereditary House of Lu' from the *Records of the Grand Historian*. The evening bath was held about six; the reader was Hironari. Same ceremony as before.

1008.9.15. Fair. Morning bath about midday. Munetoki read 'The Heir Presumptive to King Wang' from the *Book of Rites*. In the evening Takachika read the 'Annal of Emperor Wu' from the *Han Chronicles*. This evening the food and the ceremonial settings were arranged by Michinaga. Fifty meals for retainers were set out in the southern garden. About ten the food was brought in: six trays made of aloes-wood and covered in white cloth, other covers, food boxes, plates, cruet-sets, and chopstick-rests all made of silver. The Master of Fourth Rank carried them in and passed them to the women who served. Then the ceremonial dishes were brought in; two three-storey cabinets of white wood had previously been placed just inside the side door to the east. Sixty plates of cakes and dried fruit, on white wooden platters, painted and decorated with silver leaf, were carried in by the Master of Fifth Rank and handed to the serving girls; the women attendants took them and put them on the cabinets. The baby's clothes were in four caskets of white wood inlaid with mother-of-pearl, each on a Chinese table. Two of them contained three sets of white figured silk and three sets of damask; the other two contained bedding, three damask sets and three plain. In each were gauze wrappings, and they were lined with figured silk. They were placed on two white wooden tables inlaid with mother-of-pearl and covered with white material. Kanetaka,

Tsunefusa, Yorimichi and Sanenari carried these in and gave them to the ladies-in-waiting.

Kinsue, Michitsuna, Sanesuke, Yasutada, Tadanobu, Kintō, Takaie, Tokimitsu, Toshikata, Tadasuke, Arikuni, Yukinari, Chikanobu, Yasuhira, Kanetaka, Masamitsu, Tsunefusa, Yorimichi, Norisada and Sanenari stood by their places, and after the sake had been passed round they took their seats on the 'bridge'. More trays were brought in. Kintō took the sake cup and offered a poem. Paper and brush were brought and given to Yukinari so he could write it down. It was then read by each noble in turn. Then they started betting with paper as the prize; the senior courtiers and the masters also started betting. Sake was drunk continuously all the while and they began to sing songs. Gifts were presented according to rank; ministers, nobles, senior courtiers, and women of Fifth or Sixth Rank were all given presents; they are listed on a separate sheet. Then there was the parading of the food, just as the third night, except that it was repeated five times. When it was all over, everyone retired.

9.16. Fair. At the morning bath the reader was Hironari. At the evening bath it was Munetoki reading 'The Creative Principle' from the *Book of Changes*.

9.17. Fair. The morning bath was at about ten. Ceremony as before. Takachika read 'The Annal of Emperor Ming' from the *Later Han Chronicles*. The evening bath was at about four, with Hironari reading from the *Records of the Grand Historian*. At six Akimitsu, Michitsuna, Sanesuke, Tadanobu, Kintō, Takaie, Tokimitsu, Toshikata, Tadasuke, Arikuni, Yukinari, Chikanobu, Kanetaka, Masamitsu, Tsunefusa, Yorimichi, Norisada and Sanenari were all in attendance. That evening the banquet was organized by the Emperor's representative. Michikata had arrived at the mansion the day before, passing the official list of gifts on to the Household so that Her Majesty could peruse it. The Imperial Table Office prepared the food, six white trays with embroidered cloth of figured silk. The food boxes, chopstick holders, plates, cruetsets, etc., were all silver and had covers. Officials from the Table Office brought them into the garden and then gave them to the serving women, who passed them in. The banquet for the nobles was provided by the Bureau of Palace Storehouses, that for the ladies-in-waiting by the Granary, but Her Majesty's Household provided for the masters and all the others. Michimasa was the Imperial representative; he sat on a cushion at the end of the line of nobles, offered sake, and then gave out presents of long damask robes and trousers. Michikata offered a toast and the Chamberlains of Sixth Rank took around the drink. All the nobles drank in turn and soon everyone lost count.

Then there were more presents; the nobles received white robes, and others rolls of silk. In the southern gallery of the east wing was spread a purple-bordered thick mat where the three readers sat, each with his own table. After toasts they each received gifts, white robes and trousers for those of Fourth Rank, just the robes for those of Fifth Rank. Then the nobles went out on to the 'bridge', where the Bureau of Palace Storehouses had set up more tables. Toshikata gave a toast as before, and everyone recited 'For a thousand ages'. Arikuni was given paper and a brush to write down the poems. The presents for Her Majesty were absolutely magnificent. The nobles, everyone down to Sixth Rank, and the masters, all received gifts; these are noted on a different sheet. The celebrations went on for a long time into the early hours of the morning. Everyone enjoyed themselves, got drunk, and then retired.

9.19. Fair. The last ceremony of bathing. Two men of Fifth Rank acted as bowmen, standing on the southern veranda of the main building. Today Yorimichi arranged the ceremony, the ceremonial food, the retainer's food, the tables and the betting. The place settings were all as on previous occasions, except that sixty silver dishes of ceremonial food were also provided, along with two cabinets made of white wood with mother-of-pearl inlay. All the nobles attended as on previous evenings, and everything else was exactly as before.

10.16. Fair. The Emperor left the Shishinden about eleven. Michinaga, Akimitsu, Kinsue, Michitsuna, Tadanobu, Kintō, Takaie, Tokimitsu, Toshikata, Tadasuke, Arikuni, Chikanobu, Yasuhira, Kanetaka, Masamitsu, Tsunefusa, Yorimichi, Norisada and Sanenari all came out from south of the west gate and stood in line. The Office of Keys brought out the list of names and ranks and then retired. Ibata no Shigemasa and Ōshikōchi no Arimune led the guards, carrying the sword and the presents for Her Majesty. Kinsue went in front of the steps – because it was more convenient for him, he did not actually go down the steps but went down to the garden by way of the stepping stones – and stood at the bottom right. Sanesuke stood bottom left. Kanetaka and Tsunefusa left the line and joined the procession. As the Emperor got into his palanquin, Kinsue gave the order and all the bearers stood up. The procession left by the east gate and proceeded north, turned east on Jōtomon'in Ōji and headed for the mansion. Gagaku musicians struck up as they passed in front of the north gate of the mansion. The Gate Guards of the Left lined up to the south of the west gate of the mansion, and the Military Guards of the Left lined up in the same position, only inside the mansion walls. The gentlemen-in-waiting lined up by the southern end of the northern standing screen, facing south. Michinaga had previously told everyone that when the procession arrived it would stop outside the west gate, so everyone had lined up there, but now he said that it would go straight through to the southern steps, and so he asked everyone to line up in the garden instead. They agreed and so lined up facing east and ranked north to south. Meanwhile the music boats were lying in the lake to the south of the island. As the procession entered, the dragon flute was sounded and from both sides of the garden gongs and drums struck up in harmony. Kanetaka and Tsunefusa left the line again and stood by the palanquin. Two handmaids came out from the blinds by the eastern corner to take the sword and jewel. Kanetaka brought them and handed them over. The Emperor went inside and the palanquin was taken away. Then the nobles all went up and took their places, nobles in the southern gallery of the west wing, senior courtiers in the western gallery. After all were seated, the music boats departed with a few strokes of the oar. Then the Bodyguards sat themselves down on benches, those of the Left by the inner west gate, those of the Right to the south of the east wing. Yorisada was ordered to have the blinds lowered, and the order was carried out in turn by one of the guard captains. The Emperor then changed into his ceremonial robes, and Michinaga brought the little prince to him in his arms. His Majesty played with the child for a while. Michinaga then took the baby away again and His Majesty partook of a late morning meal. Tachibana no Tokushi was in charge of the serving; a number of other attendants actually set it out. After some time had elapsed, Tsunefusa helped His Majesty to change again. Meanwhile the nobles were served drinks by the gentlemen-in-waiting and others. When this was over Michikata was ordered to announce to Michinaga that the baby Prince Atsuhira had been admitted to the imperial line. The whole clan, from the highest nobles to the gentlemen-in-waiting, all lined up at the head of the Bodyguards of the Left and had Michikata convey their thanks to the Emperor. Then they performed a small ceremonial dance. That done, everyone went back to their seats.

Michikata again informed Michinaga that Tadanobu, Master of Her Majesty's Household, was to be the new director of the Prince's office. Tadanobu got up from his seat, gave a formal dance of thanks, and then sat down again. Yorisada was then ordered to have the blinds raised. The guard captain again performed this duty. Five bays of the southern gallery remained closed off as before, however. Then Fujiwara no Masatō, Takashina no Shigeyori and others carried in the imperial throne, newly made from rosewood and inlaid with mother-of-pearl, and set it up in the fourth bay of the southern gallery. They then retired down the southern steps. The throne was standing on a Chinese red brocade carpet which had been laid by Michimasa. Then Kanetsuna, Shigemasa, Kanesada and Tadanori carried in two tables and set them up on either side of the throne; they were also made of rosewood. The Emperor stepped outside and had Yorisada gather together all the nobles. They all sat on round cushions set out on the veranda. The two music boats came back in a circle and each in turn rested their oars and came to a halt by the northern shore of the lake. There was also a painted boat that was made into a stage on which dancing girls were performing – it was marvellous to see – and another boat for musicians which had a brocade backcloth. The drums and flutes struck up and there were songs and music. First 'The Dance of Ages', then 'Earth Everlasting', and lastly 'The Tipsy Dance'. Each boat had polers and boatmen who were all dressed in *gagaku* costumes. Then the nobles were given sake and food. Her Majesty's Household provided the trays and senior courtiers of Fifth Rank and under acted as servers. Cakes and dried fruit were served on silver plates which had rosewood stands and platters. Everything was inlaid with mother-of-pearl and arranged by the Household. Michitsuna was in charge and Kanetaka, Tsunefusa, Yorimichi and Sanenari served. Meanwhile the water-weed slowly swayed and there was continuous music. The lake resounded with the heavenly water music of the Yellow Emperor; the water sang the song of the river Fen. Michinaga then asked Masamichi to give the order for the music and dancing to cease; it was dusk. He announced it, standing at the head of the lake. The dancing had indeed been a marvellous sight.

The men from the Bureau of Grounds put up flares in the garden. Those on the islands and along the shore were set up by the Household. The Bureau of Grounds was next ordered to distribute flares to each boat before they receded into the distance. Seeing the boats gradually disappear was just like seeing the sun slowly set.

Then Yorisada ordered the musicians to come before His Majesty. The Bureau of Housekeeping had previously been ordered to place cushions out for them. Those who came were Kagemasa, Korekaze, Tadamichi, Noritomo, Nagatō, Tomomitsu, Tōmasa, Yukiyoshi, Yasunori, Nobuaki, Okimoto, Takayuki and Masanobu. They were given food trays and served by men from the Secretariat.

Those nobles sitting on the veranda also took part in the music. Kintō marked time, Tsunefusa played the pipes, Michikata the biwa, and Narimasa the flute. Both on the veranda and below, those who were sitting and those who were standing produced melodies that moved heaven and astounded all who heard them. Michinaga ordered Hironari, saying: 'The heavens smile upon us. The moon is light enough. Douse the flares in the garden so that we can fit the mood of the season.' So he ordered the Bureau of Grounds to take away the flares. The moonlight was bright and clear and shone on the islands and the lake. The music was soothing and after such songs, well, they call the past magnificent, but could it have ever been as it was today at the mansion?

When it was over, the Emperor was presented with three gifts attached to three branches. Tadanobu, Toshikata and Sanenari brought them up to where he was sitting, named each gift in turn, and then retired, leaving them with the Emperor's secretary. One was an ivory set of pipes wrapped in mottled blue-green gauze and attached to a pine branch; one was a dragon flute wrapped in mottled dark red gauze attached to a chrysanthemum; and the third was a Korean flute wrapped in greenish yellow mottled gauze attached to a mythical bird; all the branches were made of silver.

Then the nobles and senior courtiers received gifts according to rank. Ministers received one set of robes and a light violet *hosonaga* of damask. The Master of the Household and his assistant presented them. As for the counsellors and under, those of Third Rank and over got one set of robes, those senior courtiers of Fourth and Fifth Rank got nightclothes dyed with madder, those of Sixth Rank nightclothes dyed yellow, and the gentlemen-in-waiting and captains of the guard got the same. Servants in the Secretariat and under, clerks in the guards and above, and various other servants got one piece of silk each; the lowest ranked guards got some Shinano cloth.

Then the Emperor went inside and the nobles took their previous seats. More sake was served. Michikata was asked to have Akimitsu present himself before His Majesty. Perhaps Michinaga was being treated as head of the clan. Akimitsu approached and waited outside the blinds. A round cushion was placed in the third bay of the southern chamber for him to sit on. The Emperor informed him that those in Her Majesty's Household and their sons would all be raised in status by one rank. The ceremony was performed.

Akimitsu ordered paper and a brush which was provided by Michikata. Then Michikata said: 'Today is a day of great joy. There should be a celebration.' Everyone from the Ministers to the lower ranks politely refused, and they had Michikata report to the Emperor, saying: 'For today's events there is much gratitude. To hear again the imperial will makes his servants' backs run with sweat.' And having so reported, Michikata again said: 'There is a precedent for the Emperor's giving thanks for an imperial progress. I realize that you are being modest, but what about future generations? Shall we choose some of the Household officials and give them gifts?' Akimitsu had him relay the following: 'We may deny the imperial will once or twice, but we must follow your decrees. When we receive the celebration, let one Household official also receive thanks.' So with Rinshi, Tadanobu, Toshikata, Yorimichi and Sanenari, went Sueyori. The Empress had left the Palace for a while and come to the mansion, and now the Emperor had made his visit, all because a prince was born. The imperial favours have been greatly extended; strange how the ministers faked their humility and immediately grasped the chance of promotion!

## (c) Shōyūki

Kankō 5 (1008).9.10. At cockcrow they brought word that Her Majesty was in labour, so I went over to the mansion about six. I had sent Sukehira over earlier, and after he returned I had him wait behind the carriage. Then about eight Michinaga urged both ministers and senior courtiers to partake of a meal of rice with beans, and congee; the ministers had been in attendance there on the veranda since dawn. I left about ten, because Her Majesty was having only slight contractions and Michinaga himself told me it would be some while before anything could be expected to happen. Those in attendance included the ministers, major counsellors Michitsuna and Yasutada, middle counsellors Tadanobu, Takaie, Tokimitsu, Toshikata, Arikuni, Yasuhira, Kanetaka, Masamitsu, Tsunefusa, and Sanenari. Yukinari had left early. Kintō was not present because of the swelling in his groin that he had had for the last few days, and the new middle counsellor Tadasuke was also absent.

They had erected a white dais, with white screens and curtains, about six that morning. I wonder if there is any precedent for setting up a dais with such haste before the actual birth? About eight that evening some messengers informed us that the baby had been born, so I sent Sukehira over to see how things were. He returned about midnight to say that the evil spirits had been transferred to the mediums and the birth appeared imminent, but that she had not actually given birth yet.

9.11. Yasuhira sent word that he had left Her Majesty at about two in the morning. There was no sign of the birth, he said, but the evil spirits had emerged; yesterday Akimitsu and Kinsue had gone to the mansion to discuss things with Michinaga, but when Korechika had tried he was denied audience; there must be something behind it, he said. Sukehira went to wait at the mansion again. About midday he sent word that Her Majesty had just given birth; it was a boy. Surprised, I went to the mansion and talked to Michinaga. According to him, she had been in labour since yesterday and had been in particular discomfort from about ten that night. Today she had been beside herself, hardly aware of what was going on. But, thanks to the infinite goodness of the Buddhas and gods, she had eventually had a safe birth; his joy knew no bounds and he could hardly express his happiness. Kinsue arrived but stood outside while Toshikata passed on his congratulations; he then left immediately.

Yorisada, acting as imperial messenger, brought the sword (a large one wrapped in cloth). He came up to the blinds, where they had spread mats, and there met Michinaga. Tadanobu brought out the gifts. Michinaga took them from him and gave them to Yorisada, who then took them down the southern steps. Yin-Yang diviners and others decided on when various ceremonies had to be performed. The carpenters started constructing the bath and other necessities. Meanwhile all the nobles gathered. Today Tadasuke had another duty to perform – seeing the imperial messenger off to Ise – and so he came when that was finished. I heard it said that Michinaga presented gifts of eight horses to the following shrines: Iwashimizu, Kamo – Upper and Lower, Kasuga, Ōharano, Yoshida, Umenomiya and Kitano. The Iwashimizu and Ōharano shrines were given swords in addition. They were all presented at the Palace. There was endless celebration; seven series of invocations to the Buddhas, three sūtra readings, and I dare not record all the prayers that were offered in shrines and temples. Eloquent testimony to the efficacy of prayers to both Buddhas and gods! All the nobles were there, including Kintō, who had to be helped in. The new middle counsellor, Tadasuke, came over from the Hasshōin. Everyone except Yasutada was present. Michinaga named the three readers as Ise no kami Nakahara no Munetoki, Doctor of Confucianism (his father Arikata did the final calligraphy at the time of the birth, although Hirosumi it was who did the first draft), Fujiwara no Hironari (connected to the Lord Motokata affair of 926), and Ōe no Takachika. I heard that the exorcists had left. All of them who had taken part in the sūtra readings, from the most important down, had been given gifts of damask, each according to rank. The three Yin-Yang diviners were also given silk (three rolls for Fourth Rank, two for Fifth, etc.). Saddles were presented to the temple at Ishiyama for sūtra reading, and the same thing was done for many other sacred places. Everyone was greatly pleased.

9.12. During the ceremony of bathing the baby, ten men of Fifth Rank and ten of Sixth stood in the garden with bows in their hands; they were all dressed in white. In front of them stood the readers. For the morning the reader was Munetoki, and for the evening Takachika.

9.13. Today the celebrations on the evening of the third day after the birth were arranged by Her Majesty's Household. Everyone went, but I could not attend because we were carrying out some repairs at home. I must attend in the evenings from now on.

9.14. Sukehira told me that yesterday those with the rank of scholar and student in the clan college had paid their respects to Her Majesty. As they lined up in the garden in front of the east wing, the scholar Tokitaka had joined them. Sukehira had not seen whether or not they had received any gifts, but I later heard that Tokitaka had been given a set of robes and the others a roll of silk each. Tamenobu told me he thought that Tokitaka should not have been in the procession. I must make inquiries. I know of no precedent for the college to go in procession when an empress in the clan gives birth, but perhaps they discussed the matter informally. I must check. Perhaps they participated because the head of the clan was also being fêted; if so, I can understand it. Sukehira was in attendance at the Palace. He returned after a short while, and told me that he was not sure whether or not a messenger had gone for written permission to the Palace; the matter needed further investigation.

9.15. Went to visit Her Majesty at about six in the evening. Today was the fifth day after the birth. A banquet for the nobles was held on the western veranda of the east wing. The senior courtiers sat on the south side. Both groups sat in front of white damask screens, not at all as it should have been. Everyone from Michitsuna down was in attendance. Michinaga took his seat and urged everyone else to sit down. Then he noticed that Kinsue was not present as he should have been, so we waited a long time; he eventually turned up about eleven. Michinaga served out some drink. I still do not know why Kinsue turned up so late; everyone thought it very strange. Today's celebration was Michinaga's affair. Then one of the nobles present suggested that we ought to have some music. I replied that at two such celebrations in the Enchō era there had been no music; it was the general rule not to have music where a birth was concerned. I asked Tadanobu what he thought and he agreed with me to a certain extent, especially as the nobles were sitting in front of the blinds. But today was the day of the Monkey, so we should perhaps give it careful consideration. He discussed the matter with Michinaga, who agreed with me that there should be no music.

There were two white wooden cabinets brought in by men of Sixth Rank, six tables of aloes-wood, I think, with mother-of-pearl inlay, silver chopstick-rests, silver place settings, and silver food boxes. The trays and food were brought in by men of Fourth Rank. Serving women dressed in white were there to take them from the men and hand them to the ladies-in-waiting. Then they brought in the ceremonial dishes from the cabinets; I think there were some thirty plates piled high, but I could not see for certain. There were four clothes chests without stands. Yorimichi and Sanenari brought these in to the ladies-in-waiting. Rice balls for the retainers were set out in the garden. The nobles all got up and went to sit down on the 'bridge'. Other small trays were ordered and after a round of drinks there was poetry; Kintō was in charge. Then came the dice. Just before dawn the ministers and everyone else were given presents according to rank. Those men from the Bureau of Grounds who had provided the torches were given one piece of silk each, as were my retainers and those of Kinsue. I left at about four in the morning. For the parading of the food, seven men of Fifth Rank and two of Sixth Rank held the torches and led the way, while Kiyomichi, Governor of Sanuki, acted as prompter, standing on the southern veranda at the top of the steps.

The men present today were Kinsue, Michitsuna, Yasutada, Tadanobu, Kintō, Takaie, Tokimitsu, Toshikata, Tadasuke, Arikuni, Yukinari, Yasuhira, Kanetaka, Masamitsu, Kanefusa, Sanenari, Chikanobu, Yorimichi and Norisada.

9.17. I visited Her Majesty in the evening. Akimitsu and others were present, but Kintō and Yasutada were not. Everyone else was there. It was just like the fifth-night celebrations, only tonight it was under the auspices of the court. The banquet was the same as before. Michimasa acted as His Majesty's messenger and brought with him the presents and the food from the Palace. There was, in addition, the official list of gifts which was given to Her Majesty's officials. Rice balls were carried out and set in the garden. An extra seat was set up at the end of the line of nobles, together with a table, and they invited Michimasa to sit down. He presented gifts of women's robes. Then he left, bowing twice from down by the stream in the garden. Other tables were set up in the southern gallery of the east wing, and the readers Munetoki, Hironari and Takachika were invited to sit there. After a drink they were given gifts of white robes and trousers. Then they got up from their seats, went down into the garden, bowed twice, and left.

The nobles all moved on to the 'bridge' and more trays were provided. After a round of drinks there was poetry. Arikuni took his brush and jotted down a few of tonight's efforts. Then came dice. The Bureau of Palace Storehouses provided paper for prizes, as did Her Majesty's Household. Before that, more trays were brought out, serving women passing them on to the ladies-in-waiting. Everything was of silver: the food boxes, the plates, and the sake cups. One of the serving women whose nickname was Koma no Takashina was very intelligent, and attractive besides. Today the nobles started telling jokes and there was much drunken talk. Michinaga took off one of his robes and offered it to her. At first she refused, but after more ribald comments she was forced to accept it.

The court gave gifts according to rank. They were given to nobles, senior courtiers, masters, and officials in Her Majesty's Household. It was just as it had been in the Enchō era. Then Her Majesty gave everyone gifts. The nobles were given women's robes and either the prince's clothes or his bedding. I cannot list everything in detail. Senior courtiers also got presents according to rank. Those of Fourth Rank received women's robes and trousers, those of Fifth Rank only the robes, and those of Sixth only the trousers. Those of Fourth Rank and above were given, in addition, either the Prince's clothes or his bedding.

Everyone dispersed at midnight. Tonight the moon was full. Retainers also received gifts and Her Majesty gave all the masters a piece of silk.

9.19. At about four in the afternoon Yorisada passed on to me a note from Yorimichi. Tonight there was to be a celebration for Her Majesty and I should be present. Yorimichi was to be in charge. I excused myself on the pretext of being in ritual seclusion. I had been every other evening, but tonight was most inconvenient, so I decided to stay away.

# A GUIDE TO FURTHER READING

Murasaki's magnum opus, the *Genji monogatari*, is now available in three English translations. Arthur Waley's version, done between 1924 and 1933, with many subsequent reprintings, has become a classic of English prose and was an astounding achievement by a great scholar working before many modern Japanese aids were available. The translation is fairly free in places, however, and Waley both cut and embellished where he saw fit. Much more accurate representations of the original are now available in Edward Seidensticker's version of 1976 and Royall Tyler's of 2001. Ten core chapters have also been presented by another prolific translator, Helen Craig McCullough, in her book entitled *Genji & Heike* (Stanford: Stanford University Press, 1994). It is a measure of the draw that this work now has that there are rumours of a fourth translation in its early stages. In German there is Oscar Benl, trans., *Die Geschichte vom Prinzen Genji*, 2 vols. (Zürich: Manesse Verlag, 1966); in French, René Sieffert, trans., *Le dit du Genji*, 2 vols. (Paris: Publications Orientalistes de France, 1978–88).

Anyone interested in comparisons between these versions should start with the following articles: E. Cranston, 'The Seidensticker *Genji*', *Journal of Japanese Studies*, 4.1 (1978), 1–25; M. Ury, 'The Imaginary Kingdom and the Translator's Art: Notes on Re-reading Waley's *Genji*', *Journal of Japanese Studies*, 2.2 (1976), 267–94; and M. Ury, 'The Complete *Genji*', *Harvard Journal of Asiatic Studies*, 37.1 (1977), 183–201. A major review of Tyler is yet to appear.

For guides to the *Genji* and Heian literature in general, consult N. Field, *The Splendor of Longing in the Tale of Genji* (Princeton: Princeton University Press, 1987); H. Shirane, *The Bridge of Dreams: A Poetics of the Tale of Genji* (Stanford: Stanford University Press, 1987); R. Bowring, *Murasaki Shikibu: The Tale of Genji* (Cambridge: Cambridge University Press, 1988); and R. Okada, *Figures of Resistance: Language, Poetry and Narrating in* The Tale of Genji *and Other Mid-Heian Texts* (Durham, N. C.: Duke University Press, 1991); all these works have good bibliographies. All the other major works by women of the period have now been translated. E. Seidensticker, trans., *The Gossamer Years*

(Tokyo: Tuttle, 1964); I. Morris, trans., *The Pillow Book of Sei Shōnagon*, 2 vols. (London: Oxford University Press, 1967, reissued in one vol. (with cuts) as a Penguin Classic, 1971); E. Cranston, trans., *The Izumi Shikibu Diary* (Cambridge, Mass.: Harvard University Press, 1969); I. Morris, trans., *As I Crossed a Bridge of Dreams* (Penguin Classics, 1971).

For the historical background consult G. B. Sansom, *A History of Japan to 1334*, originally published by Cresset Press in 1958 but now available in a reprint from Dawson, Folkestone, 1978; I. Morris, *The World of the Shining Prince* (Kōdansha International, 1994); and J. Hall and J. Mass, eds., *Medieval Japan, Essays in Institutional History* (New Haven: Yale University Press, 1974). W. H. and H. C. McCullough, trans., *A Tale of Flowering Fortunes*, 2 vols. (Stanford: Stanford University Press, 1980), is a closely annotated translation of the *Eiga monogatari*, an account of court life under the Fujiwara at their height, produced not long after the *Genji*. The introduction, notes and appendices are a veritable mine of information on all aspects of Heian life and customs. Two other works of major importance are in French: Francine Hérail, *Fonctions et fonctionnaires japonais au début du XIe siècle*, 2 vols. (Paris: Publications Orientalistes de France, 1977), and the same author's translation of Michinaga's diary, *Notes journalières de Fujiwara no Michinaga*, Hautes études orientales II, 23, 24, 26, Institut des hautes études japonaises, 3 vols. (Genève-Paris: Librarie Droz, 1987–91).

Those interested in the somewhat unusual marriage arrangements that seem to have pertained in the Heian court should consult W. H. McCullough, 'Japanese Marriage Institutions in the Heian Period', *Harvard Journal of Asiatic Studies*, 27 (1967), 103–67, and the more recent article by P. Nickerson, 'The Meaning of Matrilocality: Kinship, Property and Politics in Mid-Heian', *Monumenta Nipponica*, 48.4 (1993), 429–67.